D1714325

SUPERIOR

GETAWAY

BY

TOM HILPERT

Nashville, TN

This is a work of fiction. All characters, businesses and legal entities depicted in this work are fictional. Any resemblance to real persons or legal entities is entirely coincidental, and unintended.

Cover by Lisa Anderson. www.opinedesign.com

ISBN-13: 978-1519501653

ISBN-10: 151950165X

for Jill, who gets the humor, and went to Greece before me.

CHAPTER ONE

I got into a fight with the priest on the first day of my honeymoon. Apparently, he worked at the convent that was up on top of the cliff near our hotel on the island of Corfu, Greece. Maybe, the fight was a sign of things to come, and we should have gone home right afterwards, but it was only the first day, and we both put it behind us pretty quickly. Except for that, and almost being killed by a Mafia Kingpin, it was the perfect honeymoon.

Corfu is a fabulous place for a vacation. The weather in spring is warm and mild, and each new vista seems filled with bright, blue water and scenic mountainsides. Around every corner is some quaint, Mediterranean-style alleyway with a cafe and a palm tree.

On that first morning, I woke up before Leyla, and lay looking at the bright light dancing on the white walls of our hotel room. It looked like the reflection of water. Leyla stirred beside me, and then sat up, giving me a long, sweet kiss. She leaned back.

"Good morning, Mr. Borden," she said.

"Good morning, Mrs. Borden," I replied. The wedding was only two weeks ago, and Leyla still liked me to call her that. I didn't tell her it made me think of my mother. I looked at the reflections on the clean bare wall some more, while Leyla snuggled up against me. After a while I wasn't thinking of my mother anymore.

"What are you thinking about?" she asked.

"I'll give you three guesses."

She thought for a moment, and then her face became carefully expressionless. "Oh." She sat up a little bit, and her big dark eyes met mine.

"Only one guess," I said. "You're good."

Afterwards, we showered and dressed and went out to our balcony. It was a small hotel, with maybe around forty rooms, and we were on the top floor, the fourth. We had arrived the night before after dark, and I was eager to see the view.

"Oh my," said Leyla.

Directly in front of us, maybe fifty yards away across a road, was a tiny, picturesque half-moon bay, or cove. On both the left and right, hills soared up about two-hundred feet high, and enclosed the water between small cliffs. There were palm trees scattered in front of us, and a big pine just to our left. The right-hand hill was also covered in pine and cypress trees. Directly in front of us the land was flat, and there was a lovely looking beach. There was a narrow opening in the cliffs a few hundred yards out. The water was clear and clean and of a brilliant, bright blue hue. The land farther to the right was also flat, and a second beach lay just a few hundred yards farther in that direction.

"It's just like Lake Superior," I said.

Leyla turned to look at me.

"Except for the palm trees."

Her gaze did not waver.

"And the Mediterranean architecture."

I wasn't free yet. "And the warmth." I added. For some reason, I felt the need to elaborate. "It's just like Lake Superior, except for everything but the water."

If Leyla had not been so elegant, I might have described the sound she made as a snort.

"But do you really think it's better than the Wild Turkey?" I asked.

"Better than a Reservation casino and hotel?"

"Well…"

"Don't you think it might have been a little hard for the congregation to know that we were honeymooning at a casino just fifteen miles from Grand Lake?"

"True," I said. "It would have put a cramp in the gambling habits of a number of people in our church. They would have been embarrassed to show up, if we had been there."

"Really?"

"I am many things, my darling, but naïve about my congregation is not one of them. The Wild Turkey gets a lot of business from members of Harbor Lutheran."

"Well, I guess it's a good thing we came to Greece, then," she said.

"I agree. It's very beautiful. But the Wild Turkey Casino would have been a lot cheaper," I said.

For some reason, she hit me.

~

Breakfast was on the ground floor in an airy room with a tiled floor, with doors that opened up onto a lovely patio. With the doors open, it felt like indoors and outdoors at the same time. You could help yourself to fresh-baked bread with various jams and jellies, boiled eggs, cold cuts, and olives.

"Olives for breakfast?" asked Leyla, wrinkling her nose.

"When in Greece," I said, "we should do as the Greeks."

"I don't see any on your plate."

I looked around. "More importantly, I don't see any coffee."

"Maybe they serve you the drinks."

We sat down at a table on the patio that looked across the little road to the bay. It was about seventy degrees, and the sunny air was moist, salty, and fresh. It was already late in the morning, and there were large numbers of people on the beach, walking up and down the road, and visiting the stalls and shops and restaurants that were scattered all along the street.

A young woman came to our table. She had long, dark, straight hair with just a hint of red in it, pulled back in a ponytail, and startling blue eyes. She looked to be in her early twenties.

"Hello, my name is Talia," she said with a bright smile. "May I get you something to drink?" Her English was accented, but very understandable.

"Coffee please," said Leyla, and I nodded vigorously.

"How do you say 'thank you,' in Greek?" I asked.

"I am not from Greece," said Talia. "I am El Bunion."

I looked at her, and then at Leyla. "I'm sorry, did you just say you were – "

"Albanian?" cut in Leyla. "How lovely." She gave me a severe look.

"Yes. Albania is very close," said Talia, waving her hand. "Just a few kilometers across the water."

There was a kind of sweetness about her. It was like a sort of innocence, not naïveté, but a sense that she could see the good in life and strive for it in herself. I smiled back at her.

10

"So, how do you say thank you in Albanian?"

"Falamendjerit."

"Falamendjerit," said both Leyla and I, and Talia smiled again.

"Ska jyuh," she said. "It means, 'it is nothing.' It is like how you Americans say 'you are welcome.'"

After we had been eating for a moment, she returned with two tiny cups. They looked about the right size for a child's play tea-set, holding maybe four ounces of liquid at the most. The substance in the cups was light brown and looked sudsy. I took a cautious taste, and found that at least half of it was foamed milk. I drank the rest with one medium sized sip and put the cup back on the table.

Leyla looked from me to the cup and then back at me.

"I think we may have a serious problem," she said.

I looked around to locate Talia. She was standing at the edge of the patio, serving another table. While I watched, she glanced across the road, where a big bus was disgorging passengers who were being directed toward the beach by some sort of tour guide. Giving a sudden exclamation, she rushed toward the back of the hotel. About five minutes later she returned, half-running right past our table, then down the steps, across the road, and toward the beach. She never even saw my raised hand.

"Falamendjerit," I said to her retreating back.

Leyla shrugged. "Ska jyuh," she said to me. "Almost literally. It was nothing."

I didn't think it was as funny as she did. Coffee is no matter to joke about.

We weren't bored while we waited. The place looked like Grand Lake in the middle of the tourist season. People were everywhere. To the right, about a hundred yards away, was a low wooden building sporting a sign that said "Aquarium."

"What do you suppose that means in English?" asked Leyla, pointing.

"Aquarium is Latin, not Greek," I said. "In the present context, it means, 'place to view fish and other sea creatures.' Look, you can tell which signs are in Greek because they are in Greek."

For some reason she hit me. "Mr. Smarty Pants," she said.

"Mrs. Smarty Pants," I replied. She didn't seem to think it was as funny as I did.

"I'm more concerned about *that* sign," I said, pointing to our left, across the cove. Large letters proclaimed: "Restaurant Smurfs Fresh Fish & Lobsters."

"Do you suppose they fry up little, blue forest creatures?"

"Do you suppose they serve real coffee?"

"That one is closer," said Leyla, pointing to our right. About a hundred and fifty yards away was another long, low, eating establishment.

"It's been ten minutes since we've seen Talia," I said. "Let's go." I pulled out a fifty euro note and dropped it on the table.

"Why so much?" said Leyla.

"Kill them with kindness," I said. "If we leave her a small tip, maybe she'll feel like we're even. This way, she'll feel much worse for leaving us than if we stiffed her altogether."

Leyla frowned. "That's not very nice."

"I'm leaving her fifty Euros. She may feel bad, but she certainly won't have reason to be upset with us. If she is distressed, she'll realize it's due to her own poor behavior."

"Trust a pastor to find a way to make a large gratuity into a scheme for moral improvement."

"Okay, maybe I also feel a little generous. I kind of liked her, in spite of the coffee, and it is our honeymoon, after all."

"Yes, she was sort of sweet, wasn't she? Can we go now?"

I've often speculated about whether or not that tip was what started everything that followed. Leyla tells me that's ridiculous, but I still wonder if we would have been spared a lot of suffering and fear, had I just dropped ten cents on the table instead.

CHAPTER TWO

The restaurant where we were headed was at the western end of the crescent bay, snuggled between the water and the cliffs. Like our hotel, this establishment combined indoor and outdoor space in such a way that it was hard to tell where the one began and the other ended. A host led us along a low wall that dropped down five feet or so to the rocks of the bay, and we were seated against the rock of the cliff itself, looking back toward the beach and our hotel. As he turned to leave, I said, "Coffee, please. Just coffee." He nodded, and left.

A new person arrived with the beverages, a medium sized young man with dark, curly hair. My heart fell as he set two tiny, foam-filled cups in front of us. I tossed the entire contents of mine into my throat with one normal-sized sip, set it firmly on the table, and gestured. "Keep 'em coming."

He looked startled, but all he said was "Of course, sir."

I was beginning to understand why so many Europeans appeared to do nothing more than sit around in cafes all day. They had to, just to get a reasonable amount of coffee.

After several cups, we asked for the bill. Leyla looked at it, and her brow furrowed as she converted from Euros to US dollars.

"I don't know if we can afford to stay in Greece as long as we planned," she said, handing the bill to me.

I shrugged. "Coffee is not optional. Surely you knew that when you married me."

"Yes, dear," she said, stroking my cheek. "And I'm very glad I did."

"Me, too."

We wandered along the sea wall to the front of the restaurant, and eventually, I guess, we left the establishment. The beach was immediately to our right, and we stepped down onto it. There were two long temporary docks sticking out into the bay, and several boats tied up at them. A small, thin man with a bald head stepped in front of us.

"You are here to see the caves, yes? This way, please, to the boats."

He launched into an extensive, thickly accented monologue, and we gathered that the cliffs all up and down the coast were honeycombed with caves that were accessible only by water. When one went into such caves, the water, already a beautiful blue that was more beautiful than any other water in the world, seemed to glow. The man made sure we understood that only his captains knew the very best cave, which was a closely guarded secret, and people often became seasick in the vessels of the other companies, but never in those he represented. Besides this, if we went right now, he would give five Euros off the best price on the west coast of Corfu.

With a certain amount of difficulty, we extricated ourselves and turned back, walking past the place we'd had coffee, and along to some clothing stalls that Leyla wanted to visit. After browsing for a while, we found ourselves at the foot of the hill that enclosed the right hand side of the bay. It was actually a peninsula, a finger of rock and trees that formed the west side of our little cove, and also the southeast side of another small bay. A road climbed steeply into the trees ahead of us. It looked like it might take us to the top of the cliffs, with potential for a terrific view. There were no signs, not even in Greek, and so we began to walk up the road. Soon we were skirting the top of the cliffs that overlooked our little bay. The mountainside was covered with pine and cypress and also some deciduous trees. After a bit, the road switched back twice, and then we found ourselves at the entrance to a quiet, entrancing convent.

The gate was open, and we walked along a smooth flagstone pathway surrounded by flowers and, we realized after a moment, cats. Everything was quiet and peaceful. Two kittens slept in a basket set on a balustrade that overlooked an incredible view out to the open sea. An orange tabby rubbed up against Leyla, while a calico meowed at me placidly. We wandered along a sunken path that felt almost like a tunnel because of the flowering vines that grew overhead. Everywhere we looked, there were cats. The whole complex appeared to be set on top of the cliff that looked north and west into the Ionian Sea. As we wandered, we came upon a few doorways that were barred shut, and some archways that were roped off. Beyond one of these we saw ten or twelve nuns. Some were chattering nervously, while a few were silent and tense. They all looked very young to me; perhaps they were novices. One of them looked directly at us, and said something to another of her companions, and they both smiled and gave a little wave.

A man in dark priest-robes appeared, and strode rapidly out to confront us with an angry torrent of Greek. He was in his thirties and good looking, with thick, dark-brown hair cut like a movie star, and a neatly trimmed brown beard. His eyes were almost black in an olive skinned face. They were not kind. Something about him rubbed me the wrong way.

I put my hands up in front of me, palms out. "I'm sorry," I said, "I don't understand you."

"Of course you do not," he replied in thickly accented English. "You Americans are all the same. English, English – you only speak English."

There wasn't much to say to that, so I let it pass.

"You must stop looking at those girls," said the priest, with plenty of steam still in his face and voice. "You should be ashamed! Here you are with your beautiful, sexy wife, and you can only think about those young girls who belong to God."

The verbal attack was a little bit shocking. To my mind, there were about seventeen things wrong with what he said. It was hard to know where to start taking offence. I put my hands down and stepped closer to the man. Something about him just didn't feel right. I supposed the exchange felt so wrong because he was a foreigner, and it was cultural misunderstanding. But I couldn't shake the feeling that this was a bad man.

"First, you leave my wife out of it," I said. "Second, you don't assume that I have a dirty mind, just because *you* seem to." I could barely feel Leyla touching my arm.

"What is the problem?" sneered the priest. "Is your pretty lady refusing to sleep with you? Or perhaps she is no good in bed?"

I swear I had no control over my reaction. My right fist drove forward from the hip while I pulled back my left hand, torqueing my whole torso into the punch that slammed straight into his solar plexus. The man doubled over, struggling to breathe, and then fell to his knees, still gasping for air.

"*Jonah*," exclaimed Leyla.

At last the man caught some of his breath back. He looked up at me. "You dare to hit a priest?"

"You dare to *be* a priest?" I asked, and turned on my heel and walked out of there.

We took it slowly as we went back down the hill. I was trying to regain my composure.

"Jonah, you didn't have to hit him."

"I know," I said, looking through the pines at the cliffs and the water.

"So why did you?"

"It really wasn't a conscious decision. I know it wasn't self-defense, but somehow, it still felt like it was."

"I'm concerned about you," said Leyla. "I thought you had it under control."

"I thought so too," I said. "I'll call Brad Michaels when I get back. Maybe even set up some more counseling."

We continued on, soaking in the quiet beauty of our surroundings. By the time we got back to the hotel, I had calmed down.

Our waitress, Talia, was there on the patio. She glanced at us as we climbed the steps, and then came over to meet us.

"I am so sorry I did not serve you well before," she said. "This was not good. I would like to show you I am sorry. May I guide you around Corfu town this afternoon?"

I hesitated and looked at Leyla. Talia saw it, and said quickly, "I do not ask for money for this. I think you are very nice, and I am very sorry I left you before."

I knew that Leyla was thinking about the tip. It was an awkward situation.

"You are American, yes?" asked Talia.

"Yes," I said.

"In Albania," she said, still pronouncing it *El-bunia*, "we are very thankful to America, because it was America who helped us to become a country. I am thankful to you for you were nice to me when I was not good. Please let me do this thing for you."

"You do not have to pay us back," said Leyla. I nodded.

"No, but I would like to do something for you," said Talia. "Please, it is important for me to help you somehow."

She seemed so earnest and concerned, I thought maybe it would be almost cruel to turn her down. Maybe there was some aspect of Albanian culture that made it very important for her to show us kindness. Leyla shrugged and looked at me.

"How about this?" I said. "You show us around Corfu town whenever you are going there anyway, and then you agree that you don't owe us anything at all."

Talia looked relieved. "Oh, but I must go there this afternoon anyway. So you will come?"

We had decided on a vacation with no set schedule. We had heard of the old section of Corfu town and planned to get there at some point. Today seemed as good a time as any. "Sure," I said.

After arranging the time with Talia, we went up the stairs, which were on the outside of the hotel, but covered from above by a roof.

On the wall alongside the stairway was a large painting. It was on a flat piece of wood shaped like a set of stair steps, depicting a beautiful desert scene. The stair step design gave it a sense of extra, three dimensional space, and I felt I could almost see the scene continuing on. It was strangely captivating. A small signature on the corner read "Gmac." I found that after that, almost every time we went up the stairs, I stopped and stared at that big stair-step shaped painting. It became almost a habit.

Eventually, we continued on to our room, where we sat on the balcony, reading. The air was warm and salty. After a while we heard the sound of soft tinkling bells, and then a few muted bleats. I looked up. Down on the road was a herd of about thirty goats being driven along by a young boy and a disreputable-looking dog. Leyla took a deep breath, looking at the sea and the mountains and then back at the goats.

"Could it get any better than this?" she asked.

I breathed in also. "I don't see how," I said.

Maybe, what we should have considered, is how it might have gotten any *worse*.

THREE

The Old Town of Corfu is situated on a point of land that sticks out towards mainland Greece. It encompasses less than a square mile, but it looks like something designed by Walt Disney, maybe a place in one of the parks called "Main Street, Mediterranean." More modern buildings and streets surrounded the old town, if by modern you meant: "renovated in the eighteenth and nineteenth centuries." But the old town itself was a maze of tiny little streets that were little more than alleys, and no vehicles were allowed there, except the occasional motor-scooter. The buildings all seemed to be about the same height – maybe five or six stories. The alleys wandered and connected and turned into little squares or plazas and then meandered off again. Many of them were filled with shops and stalls. We saw cafés and restaurants, wood carving shops, clothing stalls, and jewelry stores. The surface of the streets was flagstone, worn smooth by thousands of feet walking for many years. There were steps leading up, and twists and turns, and little nooks, crannies and courtyards; there were palm-filled squares and thousands of people walking, shopping, eating, and sitting at little tables on the streets, sipping the barbaric beverage that passed for coffee in that country.

Aside from the blight of the coffee, it was utterly charming, exactly what one would expect to find on a Greek island. Even though I didn't really care about the shops, with all the narrow, winding streets and unexpected little plazas, I found myself just enjoying the exploration.

"I feel bad," said Leyla. "I know this is totally touristy, but I love it." Talia gave her a wide smile as we negotiated around a group of Germans looking at wood carvings.

"It is touristy, but not fake," I said. "Yes, it caters to visitors, and some of these shops sell chintzy junk. But this is a real place, not somewhere fake created for tourists. It developed this way because real people have lived here for hundreds of years, building and changing, growing old, dying and being born, and doing what they can to make a living. Real people still live and work here, just trying to make a living."

Talia turned and smiled at me. "Yes," she said. "Real people live and work here." Initially, I was not enthusiastic about having a personal tour guide. But she had been very helpful about getting us on the right bus and off at the right place, and she had turned out to be an enjoyable and vivacious companion. It was not uncomfortable at all to have her strolling along with us.

"So what do you do for a living in America?" She asked us as we ambled through a sunlit plaza and past a fountain shaded by palms.

I looked at Leyla. "I am a journalist," she said.

"Really?" asked Talia. "Like the *New York Times*?"

"Nothing like the *New York Times*," said Leyla.

"Exactly like the *New York Times*," I said at precisely the same moment.

Talia looked from Leyla to me, and then back to Leyla. "I see. He thinks he is funny." She winked at her. "I do not see how it is funny, but I am just a poor Albanian girl."

Leyla hugged her around the shoulders. "You are a dear, dear girl. How wonderful to find someone all the way over in Greece who can help me to keep him in line."

"I will do my best," said Talia. She turned to me. "And you? You are a comedian in America, where these things are funny?"

"Now you are the comedian," I said. "No. I am a pastor."

Talia frowned and her nose wrinkled in a cute, spunky way. "Pastor?" she asked, pronouncing it *pah-stoor,* "Is this something to do with fields?"

I tried to think of a word she would know. "Priest, maybe?" I asked.

She stopped walking and looked at me. "You are a priest? A man of God?"

"Hard to believe, isn't it," murmured Leyla, her eyes sparkling at me.

"Yes," I said to Talia, trying to pinch Leyla, but she squirmed away. After a moment, I managed to capture her in my arms. She surrendered sweetly, staring into my eyes, and slid her arms around me, down my back and then pinched me, hard. I exclaimed, tickled her for a moment and then released her with a kiss.

Talia stared. "But a priest – he does not do this," she said, gesturing at us.

"Well, I am strange, even for an American pastor," I said.

She shook her head. "No, you are still a comedian."

"Sadly," said Leyla, "he is not joking. He really is a pastor. Actually, he's a pretty good one, but he is not – ah – bound by conventions."

"But he is like an ordinary person."

Leyla looked at me as if considering a dress on a rack. "I think you mean 'real,'" she said to Talia. "He does not pretend to be like someone he is not. But I'm not so sure he is *ordinary*."

I inclined my head for the compliment. "He is also standing right here," I said, "wondering if we can stop discussing him in the third person, or perhaps, at all."

"Sorry, baby," said Leyla touching my cheek. "But you are an interesting topic to me."

Even though we were already married, I felt my cheeks flush. Life was good.

After a while, Talia left to take care of some personal errands. She insisted that we meet her later on, so that she could guide us to the correct bus, even though we protested that it was unnecessary. We gave in, and parted cheerfully.

We wandered the charming crooked streets, shopping and people watching. I bought Leyla a big, floppy hat and she picked out a loose, cotton Mediterranean-style shirt for me. As the day wore toward sunset and the shadows fell long and cool, we decided to stop at a café for a few thimbles of coffee. By the time we made our way toward the rendezvous with Talia, the tiny streets were mostly empty, and the shadows were deep and mysterious. Somewhere in an apartment overhead, someone practiced a trombone, quite badly, but even that could not spoil the magic.

As we approached the place we had arranged with Talia, a scream split the air, and then a woman shouted, "Help! Help me!" It was coming from a little alleyway to our right.

When I was very young, my parents helped me to get involved with martial arts to channel my aggression. A counselor had once told me that my "fight or flight" response was very heavily weighted toward "fight." In any case, it was without thinking that I raced around the corner, up a flight of worn cobbled steps and into a deserted little plaza. In the dim light I could see a woman struggling in the grasp of a lean, muscular-looking man.

"Hey!" I shouted, slowing a little and moving purposefully towards them.

The man released the woman. It was hard to tell in the dusk light, but she looked like Talia. The man's face was indistinct as he turned towards me, but his dark eyes flashed.

"This is not your business," he said in an accented voice. "This is not America. Go away."

I kept moving, and when I was close enough, he stepped forward and threw a slow, looping right hand at me. It was all I needed. I brushed it aside like an irritating fly and hit him in the face with my own hard, straight right hand. It was dark, but I felt like I connected somewhere high on the cheekbone, maybe just under an eye. He staggered back, and I followed it up with a quick left hook, but he hunched up and turned away, catching it on his shoulder. Immediately he exploded toward me with a half-spinning right back-fist. It surprised me, but I have quick reflexes, and I caught it on my right forearm, and came back with another left, which he blocked. He followed with a straight left that caught me clean on the nose, but I was sliding backwards, and so I didn't get the full force of it; even so, it hurt, and that got my blood really boiling. The war was on.

He was as fast as anyone I'd ever fought, either in competition, or for real, and he seemed to know his business as well as I knew mine. In the dusky half-light our arms and legs were a blur of step, punch, kick and block. After the first few blows, neither one of us managed to land anything solid on the other, and at last we broke apart, panting. Fighting is brutally hard exercise, apart from the bit about getting punched and kicked. Even so, it was with a shock that I realized I was actually enjoying myself. It felt almost like a competitive fight, only with an added edge that made it even more exciting.

Dimly, I became aware that the woman was still standing nearby, shouting at us in a foreign language. The man seemed to notice her at the same time. He looked at her, glanced at me, and then turned and disappeared down one of the many alleys that led out of the plaza, the sound of his boots echoing off the walls. I was almost disappointed – I still didn't know who was going to win.

Five or six people rushed up the stairs the way I had come. Among them was Leyla.

"Jonah!" she cried, running to me. "You're hurt."

I brushed at my face. Blood was running from my nose. "It's just a bloody nose," I said.

"Here, take this," said the woman I had rescued. As she stepped forward, offering me some kind of cloth, I could see that it was indeed Talia. I took the cloth – a scarf – and pressed it to my nose, breathing through my mouth.

"Is anything else hurt?" asked Talia. She sounded angry.

"I'll have to ice my hands later," I said, "but otherwise, I'm okay. What about you? Did he hurt you?"

"No." she said shortly. "I am fine."

"When you went charging off, I ran for help," said Leyla. "What happened?" I realized with a shock that the whole incident had taken fewer than three or four minutes.

"A man was attacking me," said Talia. "Your husband came and fought him. He saved me." Her anger had eased a little, and she met my eyes with gratitude, and also a kind of surprised respect. She turned back to Leyla. "Now I know he is not a priest. He is a very good fighter."

Leyla shook her head impatiently. "That has nothing to do with it," she said, and then looked around. "Where is the man? Usually, the people Jonah fights don't get up very quickly."

"This man is also very good fighter," said Talia. "They only stop when he heard you and the other people coming, and then the man ran away."

The other people whom Leyla had brought were asking questions, and Talia answered them, apparently in Greek.

"Are the police coming?" I asked Leyla, when there was a lull in the conversation.

"It does not matter," said Talia, shaking her head. "I did not recognize the man, and he ran away. There is nothing for them to do."

Even so, it wasn't long before two Greek cops entered the square, shining their flashlights at our faces. One of them was short and broad, heavy with muscle, rather than fat. He had curly black hair and startling green eyes. The other was about medium height and balding, with a thick greying mustache on his upper lip, and cold, grey cop eyes.

Talia did not seem happy to see them, and she answered most of their questions in words of few syllables. She frequently said something that sounded a little bit like "ohee," except with a tiny clearing of the throat sound at the "h." After a while it seemed clear that the word was Greek for "no."

"Do you understand them?" asked Leyla.

I turned to stare at her. She looked at me complacently. "You know Greek, don't you?"

"*Ancient* Greek," I said. "Greek, as it was commonly spoken two-thousand years ago. And even that, I know only to read, not speak. It's changed a bit in the last twenty centuries. I understand this about as well as we would understand Old English."

"Why wouldn't we understand Old English?" asked Leyla, wide-eyed.

"Stop it," I said. "My nose hurts."

"I'm sorry," she said immediately, kissing me on the cheek. "But Jonah, why did you go charging in there? I mean, even if you were the greatest fighter in the world, what if he had pulled a gun?"

Now it was my turn to apologize. "I didn't mean to scare you," I said. "I don't know, I just don't think in those situations. My first reaction is to go and confront the danger."

"I worry that one day you'll get in over your head."

"That's already happened, more than once, as you well know," I said. "I'll try to stop it, for your sake, but it's almost an instinct."

We were interrupted by Talia. The policemen used her as a translator to ask me a few questions. They wanted me to describe the assailant, but it had been close to dark. All I knew is that he was about my own height and build, with dark short hair and dark eyes.

When we were finally done, Talia looked at her cell phone. "It is too late for the bus." she said. "The next one is a long time still. Let me bring you to my house, to my family. We will take care of you."

I looked at Leyla. "I'd prefer to get back to the hotel tonight," I said.

Talia was looking at us with appeal evident in her blue eyes. "Yes, yes," she said. "We will take you to your hotel. Please. You have done so much for me. And my father will wish to meet you and thank you in person." She gestured at my face. "You are hurt, and you say that you need ice for your hands. We will take care of you, feed you supper, and make sure that you get back to your hotel. You must let us thank you, it is the Albanian way."

Leyla put her hand on my arm, and after meeting my eyes, turned to Talia. "Thank you," she said. "Are you sure? You do not have to do this."

"I am sure. And it is not far to my apartment. Would you please come with me now?"

We wandered through some of the alleys, which were all but deserted now. After about a quarter of a mile, Talia led us up some steps to a door, which she opened with a key.

"You live here?" asked Leyla.

"Yes," said Talia. "As your husband says, real people work and live here, too."

We walked through a short, narrow tunnel lit by a soft orange light bulb, and then out into a small courtyard that held several doors. Some sort of vine trailed over a wall next to one of the doors, which Talia unlocked, and then, after ushering us in and shutting it behind us, she called out in Albanian. An answer came, and Talia led us down a brief hallway, through a small, neat living area and then a diminutive kitchen and out a large open glass door onto an undersized terrace. Everything was lovely and very old-world, and also quite small.

The terrace was lit by two orange-colored lamps. Grape vines covered the surrounding walls, and flowers in pots filled the area with a sweet, invigorating aroma. A man and a woman were sitting in chairs, sipping dark red wine. When they saw us, they stood.

Talia spoke in Albanian again. The woman came forward, nodding her head low, smiling. She had long dark hair streaked with grey, and dark eyes. The man stood, and he was not particularly large, either. He had dark hair and dark blue eyes, and I could see the resemblance between the man, the woman and Talia.

"Welcome to our home," said the man. His accent was more noticeable than Talia's, but perfectly understandable. "Forgive my wife. She does not speak English, only Albanian and Greek."

"How rude," I murmured, just loud enough for Leyla to hear. She elbowed me in the side.

"No, it is *you* who should forgive *us*," she said. "We speak only English." She glanced at me. "And a mostly useless form of Greek."

"I am Skender," said Talia's father. "This is my wife, Marsela."

Talia spoke again, and this time pouring forth a long, animated torrent of words. Halfway through, her mother began to exclaim, and then she put her hand to her mouth and turned to stare at us. Skender listened carefully, and only after Talia was done, he turned to us.

"You have been very kind and very brave for my daughter. You stay for dinner?"

"Po! po!" said Marsela. She went inside, and came out a few minutes later with three more glasses of wine, and a bowl of ice water for my hand. As I sat down and sipped the wine with my right hand in the ice, it gave me pleasure to think that since my knuckles were so sore, the other guy's face must be at least this painful.

Dinner was served on the terrace. We started with a salad of sliced cucumbers, peppers, tomatoes, red onions and Kalamata olives, accompanied by a thick square of feta cheese. I watched as Talia and her family sprinkled oil and vinegar on theirs from little bottles, and then I did likewise, also adding salt and pepper. The result was delicious.

The main course was minced, seasoned lamb wrapped in grape leaves and covered in some sort of tomato-based sauce. Roasted potatoes were the perfect complement, and the wine was strong and flavorful. The only disappointment was the coffee afterwards, but I had been expecting that, and it was far better than no coffee at all.

Talia spoke with her parents in Albanian for a few minutes, and then she and Marsela began to clear the table. Skender turned toward me. "You must let me do something for to repay you. Talia say you are a priest. This is correct?"

I nodded.

"Perhaps you like history?"

"Yes," I said. Leyla agreed.

"Talia will take you to Albania, to the ruins at Butrint, just across the water there by Saranda," he said, waving his hand. "It is very beautiful, and very interesting. I will pay for everything."

"No, no," said Leyla. "We couldn't possibly accept that."

"It is my pleasure. I wish to thank you."

"It isn't necessary," I said.

"It is not so big thing," said Skender. "You will go in the morning, and come back and sleep in your hotel same night, so I not pay for lodging. It is no problem."

Talia, coming out on the terrace after helping her mother in the kitchen, said something to her father in Albanian. They talked back and forth for a minute. He pushed his chair back, and nodded at us, and went into the apartment.

"You must let us do this for you," she said in a low voice. "If you do not, he will try to pay you a lot of money, and he doesn't have much. It is the Albanian way. This way, if I take you to Saranda and Butrint, it will be just a little money, and my time." She looked deeply into my eyes, and then Leyla's. "Please think about it. I let you talk right now." She turned and went back into the house.

I looked at Leyla. It seemed that Albanian obligations were becoming obligations for us also.

"We'd get Albania stamped on our passports," said Leyla. "That might be kind of cool. Who else do we know who has been to Albania?"

I shrugged. "It's our honeymoon. I don't want to spend it doing something we don't want to do."

"It's just one day," she said. "We have plenty of time left."

"So you want to go?"

"Oh, why not? It's another country, and don't pretend you won't love the ruins."

"I *have* read about Butrint. It's a world heritage site."

"Okay then? Just one day?"

"Okay," I said. "And afterwards, we don't speak to any Albanians, ever again, and we certainly don't show kindness to one."

With all that had happened, it never occurred to me to wonder why, in an empty plaza in the middle of Corfu, Talia had called for help in English, or how her attacker had known I was American when all I said was "Hey." If I had thought of those things, perhaps we would have avoided all the trouble that followed.

FOUR

Talia was working for the next couple days, so we spent the time exploring the area around us. A few hundred yards up the road from our hotel was a place that rented motor scooters. They were like motorcycles, only with better seating and less power.

"It will be two of you, yes?" asked the proprietor.

"Yes."

"The 50cc models get very good gas mileage, but they do not go very fast. It might be slow going up a hill with two people."

"I want to go fast," said Leyla.

"Then I recommend the 250cc model," he said.

"What kind of gas mileage?" I asked.

"Maybe twenty-five kilometers per liter."

I did some quick math in my head. "So sixty, sixty-five miles to the gallon? How disappointing."

"Do you have a red one?" asked Leyla.

They did. We rented it for the whole week, and Leyla accessorized with a red helmet. I took a black helmet.

"I'll drive," she said.

"Sure." I figured the honeymoon was a good time to reaffirm to her that I'm a secure, sensitive, flexible kind of man. I climbed on behind and slid my arms around her.

"Well, this is nice," she said.

We started out slowly while Leyla got used to the controls and handling of the bike. We climbed out of the little village of

Paleokastritsa, toward the massive mountainside on our left. Gradually, we went faster, but it seemed to me like the road was telling us to go slower. It began to climb in a series of brutally tight switchback turns. Guard rails were few and far between. Leyla goosed the bike, and I grabbed her more tightly as we leaped forward.

"Woohoo!" she shouted.

I wondered if maybe the 50cc bike would have been better after all.

We raced around turns, laying the bike far over and then straightening up for all of thirty seconds until the next switchback. Finally, we reached a straight stretch at the top of a ridge, and Leyla really opened it up. We roared through a tiny hamlet, scattering a flock of chickens that Leyla did not pause for. I spat a feather out of my mouth.

"We're going all the way to the top!" shouted Leyla back to me. I decided not to speak just at that moment.

After a few kilometers, we were back on switchback turns. Now we were quite high. The big ridge back home near Grand Lake is about a thousand feet above the water of Lake Superior, and it was clear that here we were higher up than that – maybe even two thousand feet or more. The air was noticeably cooler than it had been down by our little bay. We kept going, zigging, zagging, and racing forward on the occasional straight stretch. We came to a final piece of narrow road, going up at what felt like forty-five degrees. Leyla wrenched the bike around a curve, and then we were in a parking lot below a set of buildings. We stopped, and she whipped her helmet off, her hair flying in the wind. She yelled with joy and excitement.

"Wasn't that *great?*"

"It was something, else, that's for sure," I said, trying to quell my queasy stomach. "Hey, let me see that scooter key a minute."

I grabbed her hand, and we hiked up past a visitor center and gift shop and found at the very summit of the mountain, an ancient, Greek Orthodox monastery.

We could see the entire island of Corfu. The northeastern tip was just a few miles away, three thousand feet below us. The whole northern end was mountainous, and spread out like a hammer-head east and west, while to the south, it flattened and narrowed to its tip, twenty miles away. Just a few miles to the east, the high mountains of mainland Greece and Albania stood like sere sentinels in the sun-swept air. We turned north. On the horizon was an unmoving smudge of dark grey.

I heard a lilting voice beside me. A dark-haired Scotsman was pointing to the smudge and talking to his companion, a blonde woman in a halter-top.

"That's the coast of Italy, that is," he said, looking down at a map he was holding in his hand.

"Really?" asked his companion. "How far away is it, then?"

He looked down and then back up. "Ooh, I'd say about a hundred and ten kilometers – maybe seventy miles."

"That's not so far."

"No, a good speedboat could do it in two or three hours."

Leyla squeezed my hand. "We're standing in Greece, looking at Italy and Albania. This is awesome."

It was. The air was cool and clean, the water was as impossibly blue as Lake Superior, and the sun-drenched mountains were majestic. We could clearly see Corfu Town, and the airport where we had landed, and a myriad of bays both on the island and mainland. Our own little cove was hidden by a curve of the mountainside. To the left was a picture-perfect mountain village, maybe a thousand feet below us. We could hear goat and sheep bells tinkling through the still, clear air.

We looked into the old monastery building. The chapel was impressive with age and ornamentation, but nothing beat the view outside. We spent an hour staring and taking pictures.

As we reached the bike, I pulled the key from my pocket. "Okay if I drive?" I asked, keeping my voice casual.

"Sure," said Leyla, blissfully unaware.

I took it nice and easy, swooping wide and gentle around the curves, keeping the bike in a low gear. The only problem with driving is that I didn't have much time to look at the view. About halfway down, still far above the pristine blue sea, I pulled off to the side to pause and admire the scenery.

When we got back to the hotel, we had lunch on the patio and found that the day had become very warm. After an hour or two of lounging around the room, we rented a double-kayak from a place on the beach.

We'd spent some time sea-kayaking on Superior, and the experience here was similar, except that it was considerably warmer. We paddled leisurely out of our little cove. Some teenagers were climbing the cliffs to our left, and jumping off into the water. It looked both fun and dangerous. We kept to the right. No one was jumping off the cliff there – perhaps it was the influence of the nuns who lived at the top.

The rock at water level was punctured randomly and frequently with caves. Some of them were large – big enough to drive a bus into, if the surface were solid. Others were little more than holes just high enough above water to swim into. We followed the shore to our right, moving along the seaward side of the peninsula that held the convent of the cats. Eventually, we found a large cavern, and paddled into it. The floor of the cave was sandy, and the water was about twelve feet deep. The sun hit the sand, and then reflected upwards, turning the water a fluorescent blue, just like the boat-tour salesman had said.

"Don't you just want to swim?" asked Leyla.

"Go right ahead," I said. "I'll hold the boat."

I braced my hands on either side of the kayak while Leyla climbed out and slid into the water with a discreet splash and a small shriek.

"Cold?" I asked.

She dove under the surface and then came up, treading water. "Just at first. Now, it is amazing."

She swam around some more while I watched her, feeling hot and sweaty from paddling in the sun outside. The water looked cool and blue and utterly refreshing. "Okay," I said. "Come hold the boat while I jump in too."

I slipped out of the kayak and into the water. It was a bit of a shock at first, kind of like an inland lake in Minnesota during the month of June. However, I became used to it very quickly, and soon I was reveling in the invigorating coolness.

"Come over here a second," called Leyla. She was over against the back wall of the cavern where it met the surface of the water. Grabbing the bow of the kayak, I kicked my way slowly over towards her. "I think I found something. Wait here just a minute," she said when I reached her, and then took a breath and dove under the water.

She did not reappear. The water was sky-clear, but here, at the back of the cave, the shadows were deep and I could not make out her form under the surface. I waited a little bit longer, beginning to get worried. I couldn't remember how long she had been under, or for that matter, how long she could usually hold her breath. Surely it wasn't any longer than this. But it was. I glanced around the watery cavern, looking to see if she had surfaced elsewhere, but there was nothing.

I stuck my head under the water and opened my eyes into the stinging salt, but everything was blurry and in the deep shadows I still could not see her. I called her name, but heard nothing in reply. I was just getting ready to climb back into the kayak, to paddle madly for help when she resurfaced right next to me.

"Leyla! What happened to you? I was getting worried."

"Oh, I'm sorry, darling," she said, "I didn't mean to scare you." She did not appear to be breathing heavily.

"It's just that I couldn't see you," I said. "And I didn't know that you could hold your breath for so long."

She took my hand. "Let me show you," she said. "Take a breath, and come with me."

She dove under the water, and I allowed her to pull me by the hand. She swam straight towards the wall at the back of the cave, but as we went deeper, the rock suddenly ended, and underneath was unobstructed. We swam beneath the rock, and came up in clear water on the other side, breaking the surface in a dark space. The new cavern was much smaller, and was dimly lit by a patch of blue sand below us that reflected the light from the cave we had left.

"Isn't this cool?" asked Leyla.

It was very cool. We found a little shelf of rock above the waterline where we could sit high and dry. When I stood on this and reached as high as I could, I still could not touch the roof of the cave, which meant that it would still hold air even at high tide. In fact, I thought I could feel a light breeze coming from somewhere, which meant it must open up somewhere above water.

I wanted to explore a little, but we both worried about what might become of the kayak, floating free in the main cave. Besides, without a flashlight, there wasn't much to see. We swam back underneath the wall and came up in the main cavern to see that our kayak was still right next to us. The tide had pushed it up against another shelf of rock that stood out above the water, just like some sort of small wharf. Beyond the shelf, it looked as if there were some sort of passage back up and into the mountainside. I climbed up, and took a few steps, but it quickly became utterly black.

I sat down on the rock ledge, dangling my legs, watching Leyla as she cavorted in the luminescent water. Her body was lithe and athletic, her skin smooth and a shade or two darker than mine.

"What are you doing?" she asked.

"Thinking pure thoughts about the woman of my dreams," I said.

"Are you sure they're pure?"

"That's the great thing about Christian marriage," I said. "It's all pure, now that we're married."

Leyla swam over and grasped the rock, looking up at me. Her dark eyes were large, and mysterious. "Well," she said, "are you just going to sit there and think, or are you going to do something about it?"

My heart beating suddenly faster, I reached down to pull her up beside me. Instead, she jerked me into the water with a squeal of laughter. We splashed and wrestled and tickled, and then somehow got involved in a serious kiss. As things started to get interesting, we heard voices from outside the cave. We broke apart, breathing a little bit hard. It must have been from all the swimming around.

"I suppose a lot of people come in here to look at the cave and the water," I said.

"Probably," said Leyla.

"Shall we get out of here?"

I helped her back into the kayak and scrambled in a bit hastily, and it is possible that I paddled a little faster than usual. With my mind on other things, I didn't notice at the time that though we had heard voices, there were no boats nearby when we propelled the kayak back out into the warm sunlight.

FIVE

We met Talia at the ferry near the old town of Corfu. She seemed keyed up, and somehow not quite as warm towards us as before. Her eyes shifted restlessly through the crowd.

"Is everything okay?" asked Leyla.

"Yes, it is good," she said. "All ready? Did you remember your passports?"

"We've got them," I said.

"Talia," said Leyla, "we're going over to Igoumenitsa on the ferry, and from there we'll drive to the Albanian border. Is that right?"

"Yes."

"I read in a brochure that there are ferries that go directly to Saranda in Albania. Wouldn't that be faster?"

"It is a good way," said Talia. "But my father has hired a car and driver for you from Igoumenitsa. We will go there. Then we do not have to go on a tour to get to Butrint. It is better."

I shrugged. "We know nothing about the best way to do it. Thank you again for doing this for us."

Talia looked very uncomfortable. "No. I am thanking you."

The ferry pulled out into the strait between Corfu Town and the mainland Greek city of Igoumenitsa. The water was just as beautiful as that in Lake Superior, and the mountains were much taller than the hills of the North Shore. It was hard to admit it, but this area of the world didn't give up much, compared to our unique home on the world's largest freshwater lake. The one thing Minnesota did much better with was vegetation. The mountainsides all around us were rocky, brown, and mostly bare. It would be very hot here in a few months. I wondered if the apostle Paul had stood at the rail of a ship as he traveled through these very waters, marveling at the beauty of the creation around him, looking beyond it to the beauty of the Creator.

We disembarked on the mainland, and glancing through the crowd, Talia waved at someone, and led us towards a lean, muscular-looking man in American style jeans and a brown leather jacket over a red checkered shirt. Since he also wore cowboy boots, I couldn't help thinking he looked kind of like a modern, Albanian cowboy. I wondered if they had actual cows in Albania. He had straight, short dark hair, and wore dark sunglasses. He was about my height.

"This is Zef," said Talia, looking at us. "He will be our driver today." She turned to him. "Zef, this is Jonah and Leyla."

"Hello, Zef," said Leyla. He inclined his head, smiling very slightly.

"Zef," I said, sticking out my hand. The impenetrably dark lenses of his sunglasses were turned toward me for a long moment, and then he slowly reached out his hand and shook mine very firmly, but quickly. "It is good to meet you," he said in a deep voice. His accent was thick, but the words were clear enough.

He swiveled on his heel and led us across the parking lot. As he turned away, I caught a glimpse of some kind of discoloration or scar around his left eye, behind his sunglasses. He stopped in front of a black Mercedes-Benz. "Very nice," said Leyla. Zef just shrugged.

Talia got into the front, next to Zef, so Leyla and I got into the back seat. It felt a bit strange to be chauffeured in this way, but it left me free to hold hands with Leyla, like we were in junior high, being driven around Greece by our parents. Occasionally, Zef appeared to glance at me in the rear-view mirror, which made me feel even more like a kid on his first date. However, Zef's sunglasses were dark and his face was expressionless, so for all I knew, he wasn't even looking at me.

After a while, we came to the end of Greece, at least in that part of the world. We swept around a corner into a wide, barren valley and there was the border station – several small buildings with a little gate and clear lanes for cars to pull through. Two or three cars were ahead of us. Zef pulled into a parking space by the first building and stopped the car. Talia looked as if she were a little bit car-sick. She and Zef exchanged a few words in another language; it wasn't clear to me if it was Albanian or Greek, but they both spoke rapidly.

She turned to us. "This is a visitor center. It has restrooms and refreshments. If you will wait here, we will check you through border control. May I have your passports, please?"

"Don't we need to show them personally?"

Talia shook her head. "It is not necessary. It sometimes takes a long time, so it is best if you wait here."

She held out her hand. We handed our passports to her, and then she and Zef got out. We also exited the vehicle, and Talia pointed us into the little welcome center before turning and following Zef a hundred yards or so to the windows where a few other people were already standing in line.

We used the restrooms and bought some pathetically misrepresented coffee. "You realize that this is probably espresso, don't you?" asked Leyla, sipping her coffee-flavored foam.

"Sure," I said. "But there's only a teaspoon of it, and it's watered down with all this milk, or whatever. A gallon of this stuff would hardly replace my regular consumption."

We sat at a table and looked around. There wasn't much to see. The mountains were big and bare and brown. The visitor center was mostly empty; it was very clean and very sparse, decorated European modern, with lots of white tile, glass, and chrome.

After about half an hour, I looked over toward the passport control station and saw Talia and Zef arguing expressively. This went on for some time, with Talia gesturing back toward us, and Zef pointing away toward the Albanian side of the border. At last they came back. Talia looked angry and upset. Zef, as seemed normal for him, appeared expressionless.

"All set?" I asked as they came into the visitor center and over to our little table.

"No," said Talia. "There is a problem." She took a deep breath, glanced at Zef, and then back to us. "They have taken your passports."

SIX

"What do you mean, 'they've taken our passports?'" said Leyla, alarm in her voice.

"And who is 'they'?" I asked.

"The Greek authorities," said Talia. "They said there was a problem, and they took them away."

I was already striding toward the door with Leyla behind me.

"We already tried to get them back," said Talia.

"But they are *our* passports," said Leyla. "Maybe they'll listen to us."

Talia glanced at Zef, who shrugged, and then we were out the door.

We marched over to the border station and up to one of the windows where a uniformed official sat. There was only one, and we had to wait for two people in front of us. At last we confronted him.

"Why have you taken our passports?" I asked, without preamble.

"I'm very sorry," he said. "There was a problem. I must take them."

I stood there, at a loss for a moment.

"What kind of problem?" asked Leyla. Zef and Talia caught up with us and stood behind us without speaking.

"I cannot explain," said the official. "You will have to talk to the American Embassy. I am very sorry."

I regarded him suspiciously. A nasty thought had occurred to me. I glanced at Leyla.

"What will it take to fix this problem?" I asked the official.

A light gleamed in his eyes, and then he glanced beyond my shoulder. I'm not sure what he saw there, but it seemed to suddenly harden his resolve.

"I am sorry, sir. You will have to speak with your embassy."

"Why did you take them?" asked Leyla again.

"I am sorry. You must speak to the American Embassy."

We stood and looked at him. He looked at us uncomfortably.

"Sir, Madam," he said after a moment. "There are others waiting. You must step aside. Please contact your embassy."

I looked behind us, and saw that there were two more people waiting patiently, as well as Talia and Zef, who watched intently. I knew Americans were known overseas for being loud and obnoxious, and right then, I felt like living up to that.

"We will stand right here until you return our passports."

A look of irritation flashed across his face, and he glanced behind me again. He took a deep breath.

"Sir, please step away, or I will have to call a soldier."

Talia was tugging on my arm. "Please. It will not be good to keep asking. It will be trouble. Please."

I didn't know what Greek prisons were like, but I was pretty sure I didn't want to find out. Especially, I didn't want to find out as an American citizen without a passport. Reluctantly, I let Talia pull me away from the window. Leyla followed, scowling. Zef's face as always, was impassive.

"Now what do we do?" I asked Talia.

"I am very, very sorry," said Talia, looking it, but also looking a little relieved. "I am afraid we will have to go back to Corfu. When you are there, you can contact someone."

"Do you know who we should call?" asked Leyla.

Talia shook her head. Zef looked like he was meditating.

"I guess we could make a Skype call to Alex," I said. "He is our lawyer, after all."

Leyla nodded slowly. "I guess so. As long as we stay in Greece, we're fine, and we have more than a week before we leave."

"We'll figure it out," I said. "We'll be fine."

"Yes, yes," said Talia. "Your government will help you. I am very, very sorry," she said.

"I guess we'll be fine," said Leyla. "But I'm also really disappointed we couldn't go to Albania. I was so looking forward to seeing your country," she said, nodding to Talia.

Talia's eyes were watering. "I am so very sorry," she said again.

"We must go," said Zef, in the same tone of voice that Minnesotans use to remark upon cold weather, which is to say, bored and monotone.

"You will be okay, yes?" said Talia, brushing tears from her eyes.

"Yes," I said. As a man of faith, I try to recognize and remember the difference between tragedy and stupid irritation. I was pretty sure this was not the former.

"I am so sorry," said Talia, for the fourth time. But she was not as sorry as all of us were, just a few days later.

SEVEN

The ferry ride back from the mainland was just as beautiful as the trip going the other way. The golden-brown mountains and islands were embraced on either side by the deep blue of water and sky. The bright sun struck the water and shattered into a thousand sparkling diamonds. I knew it was beautiful; at least my head knew it. Even so, I couldn't help feeling a little sour at the thought of our confiscated passports. Ultimately, losing our passports would cause us inconvenience and stress, but that was about it. Still, it *was* inconvenient and stressful, and I couldn't enjoy the scenery as much as I would have liked. Leaving Leyla and Talia at some seats on the upper deck, I began to wander around, idly people watching.

The ship was fairly large, with two decks for cars, a wide lower deck for passengers and then a smaller upper deck for more people. Plastic seats were bolted in rows at various intervals on the outside decks, and each level also had an enclosed space for bathrooms and snack bars.

I went all the way down to where the cars were ferried. There, I saw a big tour bus. While I watched, the door opened and disgorged a tall, wild-looking Orthodox priest, clad in a black tunic over loose black pants. He must have been six-foot five. His reddish brown hair was curly and un-brushed, matching his huge, ungroomed bristly beard. He was followed by a gaggle of young looking nuns. At the rear was a younger priest, with soulful dark eyes, a neatly-groomed short beard, and carefully coiffed hair. It was the priest who had insulted us up at the convent of the cats in Paleokastritsa. Aside from his identical black robes, he was the antithesis of the first priest. I remained calm, but it struck me again that there was something wrong with the man.

They all climbed the stairs past me. I was surprised, as I had been at the convent near our hotel, by the age of the nuns. I didn't look too closely, not wanting to appear rude, but it seemed to me that most of them were under thirty. I wondered what the Orthodox Church did differently than Lutherans to be so successful at recruiting youth. However, perhaps I was mistaken; perhaps they were in their dotage, but all that holy and righteous living had helped them remain youthful. If so, I hoped Leyla and I looked that good in our seventies. Heck, I wished I looked that good *now*. When the priest passed, he either didn't see me, or ignored me, either of which were fine with me.

After they left, I realized that there was nothing to do on the car decks and ascended back into the sunlight of the uppermost deck. I moved into the crowded snack bar cabin and stood in line for some coffee. People of all descriptions sat in chairs or stood in lines, smoking, drinking and eating. The door to the deck outside opened with a flash of sunlight, and glancing over, I noticed a medium-sized man in a black blazer rushing inside, looking around as if he had lost something. If the Albanians I had met so far were representative, this man looked Albanian. He scanned the room and then, apparently seeing something behind me, relaxed.

As I waited to reach the food counter, something was bothering me, and I couldn't put my finger on it. Most likely it was the loss of our passports, but somehow that didn't quite seem to fit the little nudge in the back of my mind. When I finally ordered and looked at my coffee-flavored foam, I realized that it might have been my subconscious reminding me that regarding coffee, this was a cruel and barbaric country.

I went back out into the sunshine and fresh air of the open deck. One level below me, the young priest was laughing and joking with the nuns. On my level, just to my left, sat the big, wild-looking priest. He could look down and see the rest of his party anytime he wanted, but at the moment he was ignoring them. Instead, he was holding a little red book, and his lips were moving as he read it. I wondered if he were not very well educated, until it occurred to me that the book might not be in his native language. My lips move too, when I'm reading New Testament Greek.

The Albanian man I had noticed earlier followed me out the door and looked around, and then finally went and leaned on the rail a few yards away from me. I wandered around some more, bumping into the Albanian twice more, and finally went and found Leyla and Talia. None of us had much to say.

Back on Corfu, Talia made sure we found the right bus, although by now we knew our way around well enough to find it ourselves.

"Once more, I tell you, I am very, very sorry for this to happen to you," she said.

"Okay, Talia," I said. "We have heard you. We are upset that it happened, also. But you do not need to be sorry any more. It was not your fault, but even if it had been, we would forgive you. You don't need to say 'sorry' any more, okay?"

She burst into tears, and hugged us both, and then we boarded the bus back to Paleokastritsa. Just after we got to our hotel, a big tour bus pulled into the large parking lot near the aquarium. The doors opened, and the young Greek Orthodox priest disembarked, followed by the nuns.

"I know he acted like a jerk" said Leyla, looking at the priest. "But you know, he is a very attractive looking man. I bet they get a lot of young ladies in his church."

"Hey," I said. "I'm standing right here."

"Maybe I have a thing for clergymen," said Leyla, looking at me. She took my hand. "But for the record, I'm a one-clergyman kind of gal."

"Nice to know," I said. I jerked my head at the priest, who was leading the nuns away from us toward the other inlet, directly west of the hotel. "Do you think he is the reason those girls decided to become nuns?"

Leyla looked more closely. "It's hard to tell from here," she said. "But they do look a little younger and more attractive than you expect when you think of nuns."

She looked some more. The nuns were walking onto the beach, hiking up their robes and wading in the water. "Maybe they're novices, you know, not full nuns yet."

"Could be," I said, but something was nudging at my subconscious again, and it had nothing to do with coffee.

"What do we do now?" said Leyla, pulling my attention back to the passport problem.

"I'm not sure. I don't even know how to call the American Embassy." I checked the time. "In a couple of hours, it will be morning in Grand Lake. Why don't we relax until then, and we'll call

Alex Chan." Chan was our lawyer, but he was a good friend, all the same.

And so it was that a few hours later, we sat down on the patio overlooking our little bay. After connecting to Wi-Fi, we purchased some credits for international calling through the Internet. It was five in the afternoon in Corfu, which meant it was nine in the morning at home.

I called Alex Chan's number.

"Alex Chan's office," said a familiar voice.

"Julie," I said, "this is Jonah. Can I talk to Alex, please?"

"O-M-G," said Julie, spacing out each letter for emphasis. "I can't believe you are calling me on your *honeymoon*. What is *wrong* with you?"

I opened my mouth to reply, but her voice came through again, though slightly distorted by the Internet. "Wait. Don't tell me. You've lost your passport."

I looked at Leyla, who grinned and shrugged. "She's good," she said. "That's why both you and Alex keep her."

"For the record," I said, speaking especially clearly toward the computer, "I was not calling *you*. I was trying to reach Alex."

"And your passport?"

"I didn't *lose* it," I said, for some reason feeling like a child trying to explain to his mother. "They were confiscated."

"I knew it!" said Julie. Even the internet could not distort the triumph in her voice. "Wait," she added a second later. "You said 'they.' You lost both yours and Leyla's?"

Leyla leaned toward the computer. Like me, she seemed unsure where the microphone was. "They were taken, Julie. Both of them."

There was a slight pause. "Well, maybe even I can't take care of that right away. I think you should talk to Alex."

"You think? What a terrific idea."

"Don't get snarky with me, or I'll put you on hold for fifteen minutes."

"Yes, ma'am," I said.

There was a brief silence, and then the voice of Alex Chan came through on the computer speakers.

"Jonah? This is Alex."

"Hey," I said. "How're you doing?"

"I'm fine," he said. "But Julie tells me you aren't calling about me. You lost your passports?"

I spoke slowly and clearly. "I-did-not-*lose*-our-passports. They were taken. Confiscated by a Greek border official."

"Okay, okay," said Alex. "No need to get crabby. Why don't you tell me about it?"

We told him all about our trip to the mainland.

"And you weren't carrying anything illegal?"

"Not that we know of. And I don't know how the border station would have known. They didn't even search us, or the car, or anything."

"So, tell me again, what did he say?" asked Chan.

"He just said there was a problem, and we should contact the American embassy. And he refused to give us our passports back."

"Strange," said Alex. "If there was something wrong with the passports, he should have had you detained until they checked you out more thoroughly." He thought for a moment. "But when you entered the country at first, at the airport in Athens, there was no issue?"

"None," said Leyla, leaning toward the laptop.

There was some silence for a minute. "I don't know much about international law," said Chan at last. "But I have some ideas about how to find out. Have you contacted the American embassy?"

"Not yet. We don't even know how, at this point."

"Okay. Well, I'm pretty sure I can do that for you. Do you have a number where you can be reached?"

We gave him the number of the hotel. "You can also email us. Wi-Fi is pretty reliable here."

"Okay, sit tight," said Alex. "They don't seem very concerned that you are in the country, since they let you go, so I doubt there would be a problem until you try to leave. Most probably, the official was new or something, and made some kind of mistake. We'll get it sorted out. Just check your email regularly, as well as phone messages at the hotel."

We thanked him, and then said goodbye. Julie came back on the line.

"Is he behaving well?" Julie asked.

"I'm sitting right here, Julie," I said.

"I know," she said. "Leyla, is he behaving well?"

Leyla laughed. "I think I've got him under control, Julie," she said. "The passports were not his fault, really."

"All right, then," said Julie. "Alex will take care of this. In the meantime, you two relax, and enjoy your vacation."

We thanked her, and then clicked the mouse to end the call.

EIGHT

Talia was a nice young woman, attractive and personable, but I was starting to think that our honeymoon could use a little less of her presence. She stood in front of us at a café in Old Town Corfu. We had come back to the town to wander the streets and absorb the old world charm and generally forget about our confiscated passports until something could be done about them. We were eating lunch at a little restaurant and had received the now-familiar Greek salad that included no lettuce, but had lots of cucumber, tomato, olives, onions and feta cheese, and now, before our main course had arrived, Talia was there, and next to her, Zef. Who needed oil and vinegar with these two standing there?

"Please," said Talia. "Please do not be upset. We must talk about your passports."

Zef was still wearing sunglasses, but his face clearly registered an expression: distaste, and perhaps, I thought with a shock, a little bit of worry.

"Talia," I said, "you do not need to apologize anymore. We are not upset with you. But we would like to enjoy our honeymoon in peace now. We will get the American embassy, or someone, to help us with the passports."

"But, no!" she exclaimed, almost, it appeared, involuntarily. "I mean, I must tell you something first."

I looked at Leyla. "Talia," she said, reaching out to touch her arm. "We appreciate it. But this is our time to be alone together.

Don't worry about it anymore. We do not want you to do anything more."

Zef looked even more uncomfortable. "Please," I said, "we don't want to be rude. But we would like some time alone, just the two of us, now." I sprinkled some oil and vinegar on my salad and picked up a fork.

Zef turned to go, and Talia grabbed his arm. "We took them," she blurted in a rush.

I looked up, staring at them, and I could feel Leyla doing the same.

"I'm not sure I understand," I said. Zef's mouth set in a firm line, and after glancing around, he took the chair opposite me. Talia sat down across from Leyla. In the shade, Zef took off his sunglasses. His eyes were a deep, soft brown. Under his left one there was a bruise, already turning yellow, as if he had got it three or four days ago. He met my gaze defiantly for a moment, and then looked away. Suddenly, my salad did not seem as appetizing as before.

"Talia," said Leyla, putting on her journalist voice as she looked from Zef to the girl, "why don't you tell us what is going on?"

"We took your passports," repeated Talia.

"Why?"

"I must tell a long story for to explain," she said.

My appetite was coming back a little. Maybe I could have five or six tablespoon-sized cups of coffee while we listened and ate.

"Go ahead," I said.

Zef looked around some more and said something, presumably in Albania, to Talia.

She turned to us. "Can we move inside the café? It is better if we are not seen with you."

I looked at Leyla, who shrugged. "Okay."

Talia spoke quickly to a server, and in less than a minute we were seated in the cool dim interior of the restaurant. "All right," said Leyla. "Tell us your story."

"I was born in Albania," said Talia. "We grew up in a little village about fifty kilometers from Saranda. I played games with my cousins, and I have many happy memories, especially with my cousin Lena. Albania is a very poor country – the poorest in Europe. There is not much money there, and not much good jobs. But my father is hard-working, and also lucky. He found a very good job here in Greece when I was just a small child. We moved here and became legal immigrants. Now that Greece is in the EU, this is even better. Many Albanians wish for such a thing, but they do not get it. They can travel freely, but not many find jobs, and even less many become legal permanent residents."

I took a bite of salad, and nodded. Leyla made an encouraging noise.

"Many of the people in my country hope for something better. Many want to become like my family. When we go back to Albania, we are envied. We are ordinary here, but in our small village where we come from, we are rich. The big dream of people in my village is to find permanent work in an EU country. Greece is okay, and many people would be happy to be like us, but they really want to go to Italy, or Austria, someplace like that. But it is very hard."

I ate some more salad. The key was to get a little bit of each ingredient onto the fork at the same time. It wasn't easy work, but it was rewarding. For some reason, Leyla kicked me under the table.

"Go on," I said, looking at Leyla. "We can eat and listen at the same time." Very, very quickly, she stuck her tongue out at me.

"Because it is so poor, Albania also has a lot of criminals," said Talia. "They work together in organizations. I think you call it 'Mafia,' in America. These Mafia know that people dream of good work in the EU, and so they sometimes trick people. They say they will help a person get a job in Italy or France, and they will help to arrange everything. But when the people go, it is not good. They make them slaves, and say that they must pay them back hundreds of thousands of Euros. They make the girls – " Talia broke off and blushed. Her face looked tight and pinched. "They make the girls sleep with men for money."

"Prostitution?"

"Yes. They make other people work for them for free in shops and restaurants and places. But mostly, they take girls and make them prostitutes."

"Why don't the people just leave and come back to Albania?" asked Leyla.

"Many times, maybe most times, they take the people there illegally," said Zef, speaking for the first time. His face was grim. "The people are afraid they will be put in prison if they try to cross a border. They are also afraid they will never have another chance to work in the EU, and they think maybe there is some way to pay off their debt. And they are not all from Albania. The Mafia does this with people from Syria, Lebanon, Romania and places like that too."

"I think they are afraid to tell the police in the EU countries for the same reasons," said Talia, looking at Zef.

He nodded. "Yes, they are told they will be in very big trouble if they tell anyone." He looked a little sick to his stomach. "And the girls are beaten and threatened. They are more afraid of the Mafia than anything else."

My appetite had ebbed away again. Zef looked down at the table and didn't raise his head for a long time.

Talia took a deep breath. "I am very close to my cousin Lena, who lives in my village in Albania. We never had brothers or sisters, so we say that we two are sisters. One week ago, I heard from Lena that she was to go to Italy. She was very excited. Some people had found her a good job there. I did not know about the Mafia, about the – the prostitution. But Zef found out about Lena, and he knows."

Zef was still looking at the table, giving us a view of the top of his close-cropped black hair. Talia spoke again. "Zef is also my cousin. He is on my mother's side. Lena is on my father's side." Zef still did not look up. "He is in love with Lena," said Talia gently.

At last, Zef raised his head. There were tears in his eyes. "And I am in the Albanian Mafia," he said.

NINE

There was a long silence. "But you weren't the one who arranged for Lena to go?" I asked Zef, horrified.

He shook his head. "No. I do not do this work. I work for people who run betting houses. Many people bet, and they lose and then they do not pay. My boss sends me to – ah," here he shrugged, "remind them." He rolled his shoulders again like he wasn't quite comfortable. "But I know about the human smuggling. I know it is done. I know that the girls go away thinking they will be maids or nannies, but then they are forced to become prostitutes. But I never told these things to Lena. It is not nice to talk about."

The server came with food for Leyla and me. Neither of us lifted a fork.

Talia spoke again. "When I heard Lena was going, I did not know these things, but it did not sound right. I asked her if she had talked to Zef about this, and she said no. She said he would try to stop her. I was worried, so finally I told Zef. Then he told me all about what really happens."

"Where is Lena now?" asked Leyla.

"We do not know," said Zef miserably.

"What happened?" I asked.

"After Zef explained what happens to the girls, I tried to reach Lena. But mobile service is not very good in our village. I could never communicate with her. Zef went there, and her mother told him that she went to Saranda for a few days to stay with friends. He could not find her in Saranda, and she still does not answer my calls or texts."

"Do you think she is already gone?"

Zef just nodded sadly.

"I think so," said Talia. "It may already be too late. This is why we had to take your passports."

"I'm not sure I follow," I said.

Zef looked up. "I spoke with my boss, and he told me he could connect me to someone he knows who is part of the human smuggling in our area – at least, the Albanian Mafia part of it. But he told me that if they already had Lena, she would be valuable to them, and they would not simply give her back. We had to bring a gift, something so that they would let her go. Stolen American passports are valuable to people like this. I think they use them to make new fake passports. The ones made from stolen passports are the best – they look and feel very real, because most of them *is* actually real. I knew that Talia works at a hotel where many foreigners come, and we agreed we would try to take some from Americans, if possible, because those are the most in demand."

"I could not just steal them from your room," said Talia. "That is too risky. And it would be hard to take them from your pockets or purse. So we set it up so that you would come upon me while Zef was attacking me, and you would save me, and I would be grateful and offer to show you Albania." She looked at me. "I am sorry about your nose. He was not actually supposed to hit you."

Zef looked at me a little bit sourly. "No one told me you were a good fighter. After you hit me that first time, I forgot everything except to fight."

I grinned tightly at him. "Don't worry about it. As a matter of fact, I understand completely. The same thing happens to me from time to time."

He nodded. "You are not bad. I wonder what would have happened if Talia had not screamed at me to stop."

I looked at him speculatively. "Me, too."

"Boys," said Leyla, waving her hand in between us.

"Anyways," said Talia, "when we got to the border, we simply took your passports and paid the Greek official to say that there was a problem." She paused and looked down. "I am very sorry we had to do it, but we did. Zef has given them to someone in the Mafia in exchange for Lena."

I looked from Talia to Zef, and then back. "So, why are you telling us all this now?"

"We want you to wait for three days until you report your passports missing."

I was flabbergasted. "You're kidding, right?"

Leyla was staring at them. "So, you are telling us that you stole our passports, and now, not only are you not giving them back, you are asking us not to report it?"

Talia had the grace to blush a little bit. "No, you should report it, but we are asking you to wait a few days. I know it is crazy. But you understand now, right? This is to save my cousin Lena. What they will do to her..." Zef looked bleak, and she shook her head, as if to clear it.

"We realized that if you report it right now, someone will talk to the Greek official. He would get in trouble to admit what he did, and I think he is a little bit afraid of Zef, but he might find some way to blame us without admitting his part. We want to make sure Lena is safe before we get into trouble."

"There is one more thing," said Zef. "I do not know for certain, but I think perhaps they take the girls through Corfu. It makes sense. Greece is in the EU, and Corfu is close to Albania and other parts of Eastern Europe. It is also close to the Middle East, where they also get many people to smuggle, and finally, it is very close to Italy. Because it is an island, it is easier to come here without anyone knowing. It is a tourist place, and many different nationalities and people are always coming and going here. So I think they come into the EU here, and then they go to Italy from here, because Italy is very close. However, I do not know for sure."

"So she may be in Corfu right now?"

"That is correct," said Talia.

"Why didn't you report all this to the police?" asked Leyla.

They both looked very uncomfortable.

"We Mafia pay many policemen and officials in Albania," said Zef at last. "If the human-smugglers come through here, they will pay Greek policemen and officials too. But I do not know which ones. If I report to a policeman who gets paid by the Mafia, they will warn them, and it might be even worse for Lena."

"Also," said Talia, "if we reported it to the wrong person, they will tell the Mafia about Zef, and he will be in very dangerous trouble. They might kill him for trying to betray them like that. There is a problem for me, too," she added. "When the Greek government finds out I have stolen the passports, they will probably take away my resident status, and deport me to Albania. This will be very hard, but I am willing to do it for Lena. But I do not want to have to leave here until I am sure she is safe."

I looked at Leyla. "What if *we* went to the police?"

"It would be the same problems," said Zef. "Someone paid by the Mafia might hear of it, and then they will move Lena quickly, and if they ask you how you know about it all, you will have to tell them about Talia, and she will be deported."

"What if we mention your name?" I asked.

"Jonah!" said Leyla.

I put my hand on her arm. "Let him answer," I said.

"You can tell them all about me," said Zef. "It doesn't matter if they kill me as long as Lena is safe."

I nodded, and gave Leyla a meaningful look, which she ignored. "But she might not be safe anyway!" she said. "Not if the person we talk to is paid by the mob."

"Yes," said Talia. "So you see our problem. You see why we cannot talk to the police."

"What if we went anyway?" I said.

"Maybe I would have to stop you," said Zef. His voice and face were hard.

I was getting irritated. These people had stolen our passports, and now were asking us for a favor. "Maybe you couldn't stop me," I said.

"I would like to try," said Zef, his eyes flashing.

"I would like you to try," I said. "Anytime."

"Boys!" said both Leyla and Talia at the same time.

"We are talking about girls sold into prostitution," said Leyla to me. "Focus."

I took a deep breath, and looked at Zef. Talia had been speaking to him in Albanian. Our eyes locked, and then, after a moment, he nodded at me, and I nodded back.

"All right," I said. "For the time being, no police. But what about our passports?"

"It is what I said," said Talia. "We are asking you to please wait for a few days. When Lena is free, you can report them as stolen, and you will get new ones. Once they let Lena go, it won't matter about me being reported, and if we don't tell the police about the human smuggling, there is no danger for Zef."

I looked at Zef. "I'm not afraid of fighting you, and I am not trying to start a fight, either. However, you must know that won't work."

"Why not?" said Talia. "You say you are priest. A priest would not want this to happen to Lena."

"That's just it," I said. "I am a person of faith. Now that I know about it, I can't just let this human trafficking continue without doing something about it. What about the other girls, just like Lena? You don't know them, but terrible things will happen to them, too."

Talia looked troubled.

"I don't mind," said Zef suddenly. "The priest is right. We can't let them do this to other people, too. I never thought about how bad it is, until it happened to Lena, to someone I love." He turned to me. "I want you to report it. It might even be better to tell your own government about it. But I would like you to please wait until they let Lena go. I will not try to fight you. I only ask you, please, to wait, for Lena's sake." He struggled with himself a moment, and apparently losing, said, "But it is not because I am afraid to fight you."

"Okay," said Leyla. "It is established that no one is afraid of anyone. Can we let that go?"

I nodded, and put out my hand toward Zef. He looked at it for a moment, and then took it, shaking it firmly.

I leaned back, taking a deep breath through my nose. Leyla looked troubled. "Can you let us speak alone for a minute?" I asked Zef and Talia.

"Of course," said Zef, before Talia could protest. They rose, and he guided her out into the little alleyway outside.

"What do you think?" I asked Leyla.

She searched my eyes. "How's your intuition working? Do you have a sense about them?"

Sometimes I get these startling flashes of intuition about people, and I'm often right. "Nothing dramatic," I told her. "But I'm inclined to believe that what they are telling us now is more or less the truth. Especially Zef."

She nodded. "If he's lying, he's the best actor I've ever seen." She paused. "Are we crazy, to even think about waiting to report the passports?"

"Probably," I said. "But it is to save a girl from prostitution; plus, there is something appealing about their brazenness. And what will it hurt us to wait a few days to get new passports? At most, it's an inconvenience, and it will save Talia's cousin from a terrible future."

"Oh!" said Leyla. "But we've already told Alex!"

"Yes, I thought about that," I said. "We'll have to explain that to Talia and Zef, of course. But I think we could tell Alex to hold off a few days. He won't like it, but he is our lawyer, after all. He's supposed to be working for us."

"I guess," said Leyla doubtfully. "When's the last time you paid him anything?"

"I bought him pizza a few weeks ago. It's like a retainer."

She gazed off into the distance. "We are crazy, aren't we?" she asked at last.

"Most likely," I said.

"Well, I'm glad that at least we're crazy together," said Leyla.

TEN

We spent the next two days having a somewhat normal honeymoon. We didn't see Talia at all during that time, and I wondered if it made me a bad pastor that all I felt about that was relief. Mostly, we hung around our gorgeous little spot in Paleokastritsa. We passed a certain amount of time in our room, as honeymooners are apt to do. We swam, and out of a desire to appear manly for the woman of my dreams, I climbed part way up one of the cliffs and jumped off into the deep water. It was exhilarating, but the rocks of the cliff were very sharp and hard, and I scraped myself up a bit on the way up.

"Very impressive," said Leyla, swimming towards me when I surfaced. "Not very smart, but definitely impressive."

On the third day, Talia had still not contacted us, nor had we seen her at work in our hotel. After breakfast on the patio on yet another beautiful Mediterranean morning, we went up to the front desk. It was attended by a middle-aged lady with reddish-blond hair, a severe expression, and a thick Greek accent.

"I know Talia, of course," she said when we asked her. "But I have not heard from her. It makes me a little bit angry. Young people these days think they can take time from work whenever they want. She was supposed to be here for three days now, but she doesn't come."

I thought about Talia's words concerning the poverty in Albania and the opportunities that Greece had given her. "Is Talia normally like that? Unreliable?"

The desk manager frowned, which surprised me, because I thought she had already been frowning. "Now that you say it, no, I did not think she is like that. She never does this before." She lapsed into thought, and then looked back at us. "Was there something you needed from her? Can I get someone else to help you?"

"No, thank you," said Leyla. "We've actually become friends with Talia, and were looking for her to say hi."

"If you are her friends, you will tell her to come here, or she will be out of a job," said the manager.

"When we find her, we will tell her you want to see her right away," I said. "Ef charistou," I added, which I think was "thank you" in Greek, or maybe something about trading a donkey for a daughter. She smiled, so I guessed it was the first one.

"Let's go to her apartment," I said to Leyla. "Even if she isn't there, her parents may know how to reach her."

We took the scooter to Corfu Town and parked. After we had wandered around for about an hour, Leyla said, "You have no idea where you are going, do you?"

"I'm taking the long way," I said. "Don't you want to browse the shops?"

"It's lovely here, and I'm not tired of it yet, but actually, I think we'd better find Talia."

"You want me to start shouting, 'Yo, Talia! Show thyself!'?"

"This could be a really long-seeming marriage," said Leyla. "So you agree, you don't remember how to get to her apartment?"

Meekly, I hung my head.

"Why didn't you just say so?" asked Leyla. "Come on."

She led the way, twisting and turning through the labyrinth of alleyways. Soon we were in a little plaza that I thought I recognized. She turned and led the way up a few steps, through a doorway into the little tunnel. We emerged into the plaza in front of Talia's family apartment. Now that we were here, I recognized the correct door, with the flowering vine hanging over the wall next to it.

"See?" said Leyla.

"Show off."

We knocked at the door. After a few moments, it was opened by Talia's mother, Marsela.

She smiled and said something in Albanian.

"Whoops," I said. "I forgot, she doesn't speak English."

"Talia?" I asked.

Marsela said something else in Albanian.

"Is Talia here?" I asked again, resisting with difficulty the urge to speak more loudly and slowly, as if that would help her suddenly understand English.

She shook her head, and spoke again.

"What about Skender?" asked Leyla. "He speaks English." She turned to Marsela. "Is Skender here?" I was proud that she too avoided the common American mistake of speaking louder and slower.

Marsela said something, and looked frustrated with the situation. Suddenly, she held up one finger, and said something else. It may have been my imagination, but I thought maybe she was speaking a little more loudly and slowly. She gestured us into the apartment; at least, that's what it looked like she was saying. We entered, and then while we waited in the main room, she went to the terrace, and came back holding a phone to her ear.

After a moment, she spoke in Albanian, listened, spoke again, and then handed the phone to me.

"Hello?" I said. "This is Jonah Borden."

"Father Borden? It is Skender, Talia's father."

"Hello, Skender," I said. "Please just call me Jonah."

"All right, yes," said Skender. "Marsela says you are at our apartment? She says she thinks you are asking for Talia."

"Yes," I said. "We have not seen Talia for several days, and we were supposed to meet her yesterday or today. She has not been to her job at the hotel, and they were expecting her there."

There was a silence that stretched out until it was uncomfortable.

"Hello?" I said. "Skender?"

"Yes, I am here. I am sorry. This is not good. I am worried. I thought maybe Talia was with her friends. But she has not been home for two days now. This is not good."

He was quiet again. I was quiet too, thinking about the kind of people Talia was getting mixed up with by trying to save her cousin.

"I cannot help you, Jonah," said Skender at last. "But I think I must try to find my daughter."

"I think you should," I said. "We will keep looking too, but we don't know very many people here."

"Thank you," he said. "Please tell me if you learn anything. You can come to my house anytime, if you wish."

"Thank you," I said. "Falamendjerit."

"Falamendjerit," he said back to me.

"Ska jyuh," I said, thinking what I had done truly was nothing.

Leyla and I took an awkward, linguistically challenged leave from Marsela, and emerged back into the streets of Corfu Town.

"Now what?" said Leyla.

"Coffee," I said. "What with all this milk foam, it takes twice as much to keep up my strength."

"Oh," said Leyla. "Is that why you've been so weak?"

We found another of the ubiquitous street cafés and sat down to coffee. My expectations were now consistently low, but somehow that didn't stop me from being disappointed by the cruel, coffee-flavored foam.

"What about Zef?" I asked. "Maybe we should get a hold of him."

"How would we reach him?" asked Leyla. "We don't have phones that work here, and even if we did, we don't have his number."

"We go to Albania," I said, polishing off a cup in one medium-sized sip. "We gamble, and then we refuse to pay. They'll send Zef to collect, and bam, there he is!"

Leyla had her elbows on the table and was resting her chin in her hands, looking at me with a quizzical smile. "No passports," she said.

"I know," I said. "That's the point of this whole mess."

"No, I mean we don't have passports. We can't go to Albania to gamble."

"Rats."

She patted my cheek.

"Seriously, though, what can we do?"

And that's when Talia's cousin Lena showed up.

ELEVEN

She was a young woman who looked to be in her early twenties, like Talia. She had long, dark hair, and eyes that were so dark it was hard to distinguish the pupils from the irises. She came along the alley towards us, and then stood next to our table.

"Excuse me," she said politely. Like Talia, she sounded foreign, but her English was excellent and perfectly understandable.

"Yes?" said Leyla.

"I am looking for two people like you. You are American?"

"Yes," I said cautiously. Of course, we couldn't prove it by our passports at the moment.

"You are Mr. & Mrs. Borden, yes?"

"I'm sorry," I said. "Who is asking?"

"No, it is I who must be sorry," said the young lady. "My name is Lena. I think you must know my cousin Talia?"

"Yes," said Leyla. "But Talia told us that you were gone. She didn't know where you were."

"I am here, thanks to Talia, and to you," she said, putting her hand on my arm.

Lena looked like Talia, in the sense that they were both young women from Albania with long dark hair and similar body types. I didn't see anything I would think of as "family resemblance," but then they were only cousins, not siblings. There was something else, too. Talia had a look about her that some people might call "sweet;" a sense that whatever she had seen of the world, she was still open and hopeful, not jaded. Lena did not have that. Something around her eyes spoke of a kind of cynicism, or maybe even a hardness. Even when she put her hand on my arm in gratitude, I could see a kind of *something* behind her eyes. It was like even though she thought she should be thankful, something in there didn't give a fig for anything or anyone but herself. I wondered what sort of damage she might have suffered, even in her short time in the hands of the Albanian Mafia.

"We are very glad you are safe," I said. "That answers one very important question for us. But we have not been able to find Talia. We are a little bit concerned."

"But that is why I have found you!" exclaimed Lena. Her black eyes searched mine, switching from one eye to another. It was a little intimate, and a lot disconcerting, especially since my new wife was sitting right across the table. At last she spoke again. "I think I know where she might be. You must meet me back here tonight, at nine o' clock. I think then I will know where she is."

I broke the eye contact and looked at Leyla, who appeared slightly irritated. "What do you think?"

Lena turned to her, and gave her the same treatment she had given me. "Please," she said. "It may be that Talia is in very bad danger. You must come."

"Okay," said Leyla at last. Lena turned toward me.

"Okay," I agreed, before she could start staring into my eyes again.

~

We went back to the hotel for the afternoon, discussed things, and updated Alex with an email. Later, as the shadows began to deepen, we went back to Corfu Town.

As we had seen before, by nine o'clock at night, the narrow alleys and byways were practically deserted. The café where we had met Lena earlier was an oasis of soft, warm light spilling out onto the empty street. Lena stepped swiftly out of the darkness and intercepted us before we reached the doorway.

"Come quickly!" Her voice was urgent, and she pulled on my arm. "Talia is in great danger. You must come right away."

"Where is she?" I asked.

"Come," she said. "Hurry."

Still holding my arm, she guided us rapidly through a series of dizzying twists and turns, up stairways and through short tunnels. After the time we had spent here, I thought I had known the old town of Corfu pretty well, but I was lost within five minutes. At last we crossed what seemed to be a more normal street, one with a blacktop surface, painted lines, and actual motor vehicles traveling on it. We turned into another alley, and went through a noisy stretch where there were several bars and lots of people out in the street. After another corner, Lena guided us up five steps to a doorway. There was a small sign hanging above the door with a suggestive picture of a woman on it. I recognized a form of the Greek word for "house" on the lettering of the sign, but couldn't get any more than that.

Lena released my arm and looked at us. "She is in here. You must come with me."

"Okay," I said. As Lena turned to knock on the door, I looked at Leyla. She nodded quickly at me.

"Is there a bathroom in there?" asked Leyla. "I really need one."

Lena gave her a distracted look. "Yes, of course."

The door opened in response to her knock. A big, dark-haired man stood there. When he saw Lena, he stepped aside and gestured us in. I took a hasty step forward, tripped, and fell into the man. Instinctively, he tried to hold me up, but our legs got tangled, and we both stumbled, at last falling in a heap a few feet inside the door.

He twisted quickly, putting a hand on my throat as I lay face up. Lena spoke to him sharply in a foreign language, and after a slight hesitation, he released me, and climbed back to his feet, leaving me on the floor. I held out my hand for help up, but he ignored it, saying something to Lena as he closed the door. I got up, unassisted, and dusted myself off.

"Sorry," I said.

The room was dimly lit, and furnished in European modern, which, to me, meant clean, but cold and uncomfortable. Thick red curtains covered the windows. Lena was speaking to a heavily made-up woman wearing stylish, but very tight clothing. She might have been middle-aged. She might have been attractive, but it was hard to tell in the dim light and with all the make-up.

To my left was a long, low yellow couch. Three young women sat there, smoking, two of them reading magazines, the other staring off into space with hollow eyes, as if her mind was somewhere far away, while the smoke drifted unnoticed in front of her. The air was thick with a miasma of cheap perfume, cigarette smoke, and other, even less pleasant, odors. The girls all wore short silk robes. Two of them had stockings on their legs that stopped mid-thigh, held up with straps that went up under their robes. In the gaps of the robes I caught glimpses of lacy undergarments. In short, they were obviously prostitutes. It seemed like seeing those women half-dressed like that should get me excited, and maybe in a way, at first, it did, but it was more surprise than anything else, and it quickly wore off into something depressing and even mildly revolting. The girls wore the skimpy clothes like any mechanic wears coveralls. They were at work, wearing the uniform, just taking a break. In my worldview, admittedly, not shared by all, sex is a kind of holy gift shared between God and married couples. Even a lot of people who aren't specifically Christian seem to agree that sex ought to at least be accompanied by love. But here, somehow, those girls sitting on the couch half-undressed, taking a smoke break, reduced it to a meaningless business transaction associated with a basic bodily function; kind of like paying to go to the toilet and making a big deal out of it. The cheapness, the shallowness, the emptiness of it all was painfully self-evident, even while the lingerie tried to dress it up as something exciting.

The big man glanced at me once, picked up a magazine of his own and sat in a square red armchair across from the girls. Lena turned toward me, then glanced around the room.

"Where is your wife?" She asked.

"I don't know," I said. Leyla was nowhere to be seen. "She had to go to the bathroom. That's probably where she is."

Lena turned back to the middle-aged woman and spoke again. She in turn raised her voice, toward the big man I had run into. He grunted and replied, clearly in the negative. Lena and the woman spoke again, and then ended with shrugs.

"Just have them tell Leyla where to go when she comes out," I said. "Let's not waste any time. You said Talia was in danger." Seeing that we were in a brothel, I had a sick feeling about the sort of trouble she was in.

Lena hesitated, shrugged again and led the way down a short hallway.

The room she brought me to was a small office. "Wait here," said Lena, and shut the door.

At one end was a desk with a closed laptop computer in the middle of it. The rest of the surface was clean and free of clutter. Two leather chairs were ranged in front of the desk, and two more were clustered together in front of a window, with a lamp between them. The wall behind the desk held a bookshelf with very few books, and some sort of framed, official-looking document in Greek. The other wall was covered in high quality, clearly posed pictures of women in various stages of undress. The walls holding the window and door were similarly decorated. I stood and looked at the closed blinds of the window.

Thankfully, it wasn't long before the door opened again. I stood to the side, and a large, heavy-set middle-aged man wearing a suit entered. He had dark hair, dark cold eyes, and that strange mix of Slavic and Mediterranean features that I was learning was typical of Albanians. Something else about him looked familiar, but I couldn't place it. He was followed by a younger man wearing tight jeans and a tight leather jacket over a white muscle shirt. He also looked Albanian.

The older man glanced at me, and then, with a small groan, sat behind the desk. I could see that he had an ugly scar running from the right corner of his mouth for several inches toward his ear. When he was settled, he looked at me more directly. "Father Borden," he said in accented English. "I am happy you came to see me. My name is Yakov," he said. He waved a hand at the other man. "This is Bekim." Bekim stood silently, his right hand holding his left in front of him, like a soldier in the 'at ease' posture.

"I'm not sure what this is about," I said carefully. "I did not actually come to see you. I came to find a friend of mine."

"Ah, yes," said Yakov. "Your friend, Talia." He sighed and contemplated one of the pictures on the wall to his right. "You have known her long?"

"Actually, no," I said.

"I see." He looked back at me. "I must tell you, it is not always safe for Americans on holiday to make friends with foreigners. Many people make scams."

"I'm sure they do," I said. I waited. Yakov waited. After a long few moments, he leaned forward in his chair.

"Ah, so? You are perhaps a more interesting man than I thought, Father Borden. You do not talk to fill the silence?"

After that, I felt it would be gauche to say something to fill the silence, so I simply nodded and waited some more. Yakov leaned back in his chair and chuckled. "Yes, you are unusual, especially for a priest. I think perhaps I could even like you."

Bad guys are always saying things like that to me. I wondered if it ever occurred to them that most people were not happy to have the approval of scum-of-the-earth types. If I was the sensitive kind, I might have even considered it an insult.

"You were going to tell me about Talia?" I said at last.

Yakov slowly shook his head. "You must forget Talia," he said. "She has told you a long fairy-story."

I thought about that some more. It's true that we didn't know Talia. But after being a pastor for ten years, I did know *people*, in general. It was actually one of my best things – I often had kind of an intuitive sense about people and situations. I had believed Talia. I thought about our conversations. I thought about meeting her family. Finally I looked back at Yakov.

"It was a nice story," I said. "I liked it."

He smiled, but it didn't touch his bleak eyes. "Yes, she is a very good story-teller," said Yakov. "But you do not know her. You must not believe everything she says."

"I do not know you, either."

A momentary flash of ugly rage surged in his dark eyes, and then he had it under control. But I knew I had seen it, and it made me even less inclined to trust him.

"Father Borden, listen to me. You must forget Talia. She has sold your passports and gone back to her village in Albania. Her father sent her away to get married. It is how we do things in Albania."

The hair on the back of my neck prickled. Obviously, Yakov did not know I had met Talia's parents and spoken with them recently. There was no reason he should. But now I knew for certain he was lying to me. The question is, who was he, and what did he gain if I quit looking for Talia?

"Why do you care that I am looking for Talia?" I asked.

He sighed, to show me how patient he was being. "I am a friend of the family. Her father asked me to speak with you, to explain. There is no need to go on asking about her. She is in Albania."

"What about Lena?"

"There is no Lena. Talia made her up so you would give her the passports. The girl who brought you here is called Besa."

That hit me like a straight punch to the stomach. I thought the Lena situation was resolved, but now, if there *was* a Lena, obviously, she was still captive to the Albanian mob.

"How did you know about my stolen passports?" I asked.

"Her father."

I hesitated. It didn't sound like Skender, and Skender could have told me all this himself when I spoke to him, earlier. Yet, it seemed like Yakov did know, after all, that I had met Talia's family. It was just possible that he was telling the truth. I didn't think so, but it was possible. I had two choices at that moment. I could confront Yakov then and there, or I could gather more information, and maybe send the police after him. After all, the man was apparently running a brothel, and he didn't seem very careful about who knew it.

"You are a pimp?"

His voice was cold. "I am a businessman. Men will pay for this," he waved his hand at the pictures on the wall, "so why should I not be the one they pay?"

"Because you aren't the one doing the – ah – work?"

"You are foolish," said Yakov. "There is always a man behind the girls in this work. No woman does this on her own. There is always a man somewhere near to provide protection, and, shall we say, to encourage her to keep up the good job." He chuckled as if he had said something funny.

"And to cash in."

"I am like any employer. The owner always makes more money than the workers. I provide a valuable service to these girls. I give them a place to work that is safe. I pay for this house, not them. I protect them from men who might hurt them."

I could feel a kind of tightness in my head. "And who protects them from you?"

Yakov's face darkened, and his mouth tightened into a hard, straight line. "Get out," he said. "I have tried to be reasonable. If you look for Talia any more, you will not find her. You will find only trouble. Now, get out!"

He spoke sharply to Bekim, who moved towards me. I eyed him, and finally decided that as much as I wanted to hit someone, punching him would serve no real purpose. I turned toward the door. Bekim followed me all the way down the hall and opened the outside door for me.

I went down the steps to the street and took a deep breath. After the brothel, the air seemed fresh and clean, and I could taste the salt-soft scent of the sea on the breeze. Though I was somewhat lost, I had a general sense of where I was, and I remembered the last two turns we had taken, so I walked slowly back the way we had come. About two hundred yards along the street, I noticed a beautiful woman sitting at a café table on the sidewalk. She had dark hair tumbling in waves to the middle of her back, and smooth, slightly dark skin, like a lot of the Mediterranean people I had seen in

Greece. Her eyes were large and almond shaped, and regarded me with frank interest. I sat down at the table across from her.

"Hello, Gorgeous," I said. "Will you marry me?"

"I just did," she said. "Two weeks ago."

"Well that makes it less complicated," I said.

"Jonah," said Leyla, "What happened in there?"

"Well, first off," I said, "our little plan went brilliantly. No one saw you disappear. They're probably still waiting for you to come out of the bathroom."

"Was it all really necessary?"

"Well," I said, "obviously not in retrospect. Still, I think it was the smart thing to do. If they had planned something nasty, you would have gone to the police and known right where I was."

"Waiting was a little tense. I know you said wait for a whole hour before going to the police, but even just these twenty minutes were kind of tough."

"Well, I'm glad you weren't in there with me," I said. "It was a brothel."

There was an awkward pause. "You know," said Leyla diffidently, "there could be several reasons why you would be glad your wife wasn't with you when you went to a brothel."

I took her hand. "You've got nothing to worry about, Baby," I said. "Being monogamous with you is a small price to pay for something as wonderful as being with you at all."

A smile filled her face. "You are very sweet. And so eloquent."

"Well, I'm paraphrasing Chesterton," I said.

"I didn't know he felt that way about me."

I looked up to the heavens. "I don't know why I bother."

She grabbed my hand. "Yes, you do. We both do."

I met her eyes. "Yes, I guess we do."

We ordered coffee, which was not as fun as it might have been, and I told her all about my conversation with Yakov.

"What do you think?" I asked when I was done.

"I wasn't there," said Leyla. "But what about Zef? If there is no Lena, what was he doing in the middle of all this?"

"I wondered the same thing," I said. "Could he be in love with Talia?"

Leyla shook her head. "No. I think both of us would have picked up on that vibe. Yakov didn't mention him?"

"No. And I didn't want to bring him in to the conversation, because if Yakov is up to no good, Zef could be a wild card in our favor."

"The man runs a brothel. Of course he's up to no good."

"You know what I mean – if he's done something to Talia."

She nodded. "Zef could also get himself in real trouble if the mob finds out that in this situation he's working against them, instead of for them."

"That thought had also occurred to me."

"So what do we do?"

"We finish this swill," I said, pointing to the coffee, "and go back to the hotel and go to bed."

"And after that?"

I looked at her steadily, and finally she blushed a little and smiled.

"I meant, tomorrow."

"Honestly, I don't know," I said.

"Well, the first part of the plan was pretty good anyway," she said.

TWELVE

The next morning we emailed Alex Chan. Talia's plan had apparently failed, and we wanted to get the ball rolling our passports right away. It was still night time back in Grand Lake, but it was all we knew to do, and at least he would get the message first thing in the morning. After that, there didn't seem to be much that we could do.

It was our honeymoon after all, so, we had a leisurely breakfast, and sat around on our balcony reading for a while, pausing every so often to admire the exotic view.

We went swimming again, and had a nice lunch that contained, as far as we could tell, no Smurfs. In the middle of the afternoon, Leyla put down her book, a history of the 1840 US presidential election by Mark Cheathem. "I can't take it anymore!" she said.

"I'm so glad you said that," I said quickly. "We can't just leave it all like this. We know about a brothel. We think we know about human trafficking, and a girl we know is missing. We have to do something."

"I was talking about the events in this book," said Leyla. "The politics back then were as nasty as they are today – maybe even worse." She made a placating gesture. "But I agree with you. All that is really bothering me as well. I was putting it off, but you're absolutely right – we have to do *something*."

"What do you think?"

"Go to the police?"

"Yes," I said. "But maybe first we should check Yakov's story, just to make sure that Talia really is missing. We should talk to her father again. If he says she's missing, we go to the cops."

"If she is, won't Skender have already done that by now?"

"Maybe. If so, he'll tell us, and then we'll know it's done. But I need to know for sure."

"Sounds good to me."

It was getting on toward evening when we made our way back to Talia's apartment in Corfu Town. After knocking, we stood outside the door for a long time. We could hear the muted murmur of all the people in the narrow streets nearby, but the courtyard where we stood was quiet and deserted. No one came to the door, no matter how many times we knocked.

"Now what?" asked Leyla.

"Coffee," I said firmly. "Then we regroup."

At a nearby café, I tried to look suave and bored like the other Europeans around us, but I was keyed up. "Let's do this," I said. "When we're done here, you go to the police. I'll go back to Talia's house and see if anyone has come home. Either way, I'll wait there for you and the cops to show up."

"Won't they be mad, if it's all a false alarm?"

"That's why you go by yourself. They won't be as inclined to be so angry at a beautiful young woman."

She smiled. "You're pretty smooth, aren't you?"

"Just call me 'Slick.'"

"No," she said. "I won't. But I will go get the police."

She left while I paid for the coffee, wondering, as always if it was worth it. Afterwards, I made my way back to the apartment where

Talia lived with her family. As I reached the door, a man emerged from the short tunnel into the courtyard behind me. When I turned to look at him, two more men had followed him.

I knocked at Talia's door, and pulled off a piece of vine, fiddling with it while I waited. Glancing over my shoulder, I saw that the three men had spread out and were all approaching me from different directions. With no answer coming from Talia's apartment, I turned, putting my back to the door, looking at the men.

They all wore dark jeans, and t-shirts under dark blazers. It looked almost like a uniform. One of the men looked vaguely familiar. After a moment, I realized he was the big man I had bumped into in Yakov's brothel. I plucked another piece of vine and nervously twisted the pieces in my hands as they approached.

"What can I do for you fellas?" I asked.

No one replied. They were not a talkative bunch. At last, they stopped in a little semi-circle in front of me.

"You must come with us," said the big man I recognized, in a thick, barely understandable accent.

"Why is that?" I asked, looking down at the vine I was still twisting in my hands.

"Yakov want you," said the thug in front of me.

"Well, then," I said, "why didn't you just say so?"

The big man looked puzzled "I say so. Right now." I shook my head. Thugs are notorious for not having much of a sense of humor. Though, to be fair, maybe the guy was a scream to hang out with in his own language.

"Okay then," I said, tossing my little piece of vine in front of the door to Talia's family apartment, hoping I hadn't messed it up too badly, "Let's go."

The big man led the way, and the two others fell in behind me. They took me through the narrow streets as darkness was falling, and out of the Old Town, to the house I had been in the night before, the brothel.

The big man put me back in the office and then left me alone with all the pictures of naked, and partially naked, women. I stood looking at the closed curtains of the windows. Time passed, and no one came in. I went to the door, but found it was locked from the outside. I waited some more. I was starting to get irritated, which is a problem I have from time to time.

I caught myself looking at some of the pictures that covered the walls, and it occurred to me that I might spend the remainder of my wait in a very enjoyable fashion. I went ahead with it. Even so, eventually, I found myself with nothing to do once more. I was contemplating the window again, this time to try and exit through it, when the door opened, and Yakov walked in, followed by his bodyguard from the previous night, Bekim. He stopped and stared at the room around him, and then whirled on me.

"What is this?" he shouted. "What have you done?"

Bekim was looking around at the room and shaking his head.

"I was tired of looking at the window, and I didn't want to look at your pictures of naked girls, so I did a little redecorating," I said, looking around with satisfaction. "I've really spruced the place up, don't you think?"

My enjoyable activity had been to pull every single picture of the girls off the walls, tear them into small pieces, and throw them on the floor. I felt it was time well spent.

"You – you – "

I waited while he sputtered in rage. "I know English is not your primary language," I said, "but maybe you should work on your vocabulary."

Yakov finally found his voice again, but his vocabulary was still quite repetitive, and I noticed a marked tendency to use only certain types of words.

I thought maybe he would try to hit me, which would have been very satisfying for me, since I would have almost been obligated to hit him back, but at the last minute, he pulled up and stood staring at me with snapping dark eyes. I met his gaze calmly, and finally he turned his head and barked an order at Bekim in Albanian. Bekim nodded and left the room.

"I see I am going to have to make it very clear to you," said Yakov. He was under control now, but obviously, still raging inside. Very deliberately, he sat down in one of the leather chairs by the window. He did not invite me to sit.

The door opened, and a girl came in, followed by Bekim, who closed it again. The girl had big dark eyes, long black hair, and not much of her body covered. She wore too much make-up, too much perfume, and she was as skinny as an addict, with just about as much charisma. Her eyes were hollow and dead.

"This is Reza," said Yakov. "Reza belongs to me."

"She may work for you," I said, "but she belongs to God."

"No, this is what I tell you," said Yakov slowly and clearly. "She is mine. All the girls are mine. Your god is nobody. *I* am their god."

He turned to Reza who was standing, looking at nothing. "Reza speaks a little bit of English. Don't you, Reza?"

She nodded.

"Am I your god, Reza?" he asked.

"Yes, sir," she said. Her voice did not seem to carry much emotion.

"Your god tells you to clean up this mess," he said, waving his arm at the pieces of photographs scattered all over the room. She immediately began to brush the fragments off the furniture, and then, lacking a broom, she got down on her hands and knees to sweep them into a pile on the floor. Some people might have thought a girl cleaning in her lingerie was sexy, but it just made her look humiliated and pathetic. I felt sick to my stomach.

"Stop it," I said.

Yakov turned to me with vindictive triumph in his eyes. "Really, Father Borden? But you were the one who made the mess. It is your fault she has to clean."

"Stop it," I said evenly.

"Very well," said Yakov. "Reza, leave that for now. Come over here."

Reza turned and began to get to her feet. "I did not tell you to stand," said Yakov sharply. Without hesitation, Reza returned to her hands and knees and began to crawl towards him with an exaggerated sway to her hips and a look on her face that was presumably supposed to be sexy.

"All my girls belong to me, like Reza here. I worked hard to get them. They are mine. Do you understand now?"

"Why are you telling me this?" I asked, barely in control of my voice.

"Your little friend Talia with all her years here in Greece forgot her place. Albanians do not interfere with me and my property. Her cousin was mine. I got her. I will do as I please with her. But Talia tried to take my property away from me. I cannot tolerate this, and not from a *girl* of all people! So now Talia is mine, too."

"So Lena is real, and Talia was not sent away to get married."

"That is right. Those two girls belong to me, now. You must stop interfering with my property."

"No," I said.

"Let me demonstrate to you, Borden," said Yakov. "I have been on my feet all day long. They are tired and sweaty." He looked back at Reza who was now next to his chair, still on her hands and knees, waiting expectantly. "Take off my shoes," he said.

The moment she pulled them off, the powerful, rank odor of stinking feet wafted throughout the room. It overwhelmed even the cheap perfume worn by Reza.

"Now the socks," said Yakov.

Though I hadn't thought it possible, when Reza removed his socks, the smell grew even worse. This man had a serious foot odor problem. Fitting, I thought, for a glorified pimp.

Yakov met my eyes. Without looking away, he said to Reza, "Clean my feet."

My eyes jerked away in horror as I saw Reza flatten herself to the floor and start licking his feet.

"Stop it," I said. I could barely control my voice.

"As you wish," he said. He kicked Reza in the face and she sprawled on the floor.

She got back to her hands and knees, licking the blood that was dripping from her nose.

"This is what Talia will become. And this is what I will do to your pretty little wife if you do not leave it all alone and go home to America where you belong."

I was moving well before he had finished talking. My first punch broke his nose, for which I was grateful, at least until I felt guilty, later. After that, Bekim was on me, and I didn't have any more time to spare for Yakov. Like a lot of tough guys, Bekim probably spent much more time working out in the gym and looking tough on the job than actually fighting people. His first mistake was to grab me with his left hand, intending to pull me around to meet his right hand. Since I was already bent low after hitting Yakov in the chair, I came around as he pulled me, but stayed low. As his right hand whistled over my head, I swept his legs out from under him, and drove a knee into his solar plexus right about the time he hit the ground. I followed with a left and then a right on his undefended temples, and then quit. The wind had been knocked out of him, and his eyes were rolled back, and I didn't want to kill him.

Reza remained kneeling on all fours, just as she had been, blood still trickling from her nose where Yakov had kicked her.

"Get up," I said, taking her arm, and helping her to her feet. I stepped to where Yakov sat dazed in his chair, cradling his face while a considerable amount of blood flowed from his nose. He offered no resistance as I pulled open his suit coat, and ripped out a piece of the silk lining, handing it to her. Without a word, she put it to her face.

"Get out of here," I said. "Go. The police are coming. You are free now." She stood without moving, staring at Yakov. "Go," I said. "Hurry now." I gave her a little push, and at last she stumbled from the room in a daze.

I turned to Yakov. "You are not much of a god. I have taken her from you. And I will take Talia from you also." I was almost shaking with rage. "The fact that you are still alive is proof that *my* God exists. If it were not for him, I would break every bone in your body and then dump you into the ocean like a piece of garbage."

Yakov tried to say something, and coughed violently, spitting blood onto his clothing. He finally croaked, "Yes, I am alive. But I have no god to restrain me, and you are a dead man."

"Alive or dead, I belong to my God. If I were you, I'd start thinking about that."

Yakov began to struggle to sit more upright. I thought I'd like to cheer him up some more.

"By the way, the police should be here any minute now." I hoped it was true. I hoped Leyla had understood my message.

A light gleamed in his eyes, which seemed a little strange to me. He relaxed and leaned back in his chair, breathing through his mouth. Yakov's bodyguard, Bekim, began to groan, and slowly rolled up to his hands and knees. I looked at him.

"I don't like your choice of employer," I said to him, "but I have no quarrel with you. I'm done if you are." He looked at me, and nodded his head twice. He was going to be groggy for some time to come.

Within fifteen minutes, my hopes proved well-founded. I could hear a group of people in the street outside the window, and a few minutes later, there was a knock at the door of the office. I opened it to admit three men wearing police uniforms. They looked more or less like American police uniforms. Behind them was Leyla. She pushed through them and rushed into my arms.

"Thank goodness!" she said. "I saw the little vine that you twisted into a Y-shape and left outside Talia's door, but it took me some time to convince the police to come here."

The cops were looking around the room. Reza had not finished cleaning up the shreds of the photographs that I had destroyed. Bekim was still on his hands and knees, and Yakov still in his chair, although he had stopped bleeding.

One of the cops was a short, trim, gray-haired man. He looked around and then said in English, "What is going on here?"

"This man is running a brothel in this house," I said, pointing to Yakov. "If you simply look around the rest of the house, you will see it. I think some of the girls are here against their will."

The gray-haired cop turned and looked at me with steel-gray eyes. "We *know* this man runs a brothel. That is his business. There is his license, on the wall." He pointed to the official looking document that hung in a frame behind the desk.

"What do you mean? Do you mean prostitution is *legal* here?"

The cop shook his head in disapproval. "You Americans think you know better than everyone else. Yes, prostitution is legal in Greece. This man has a license for this establishment. The people who work here are registered sex-workers. It is not your business to stop him, just because you don't like it. This is not America."

I was at a loss for words, surprised and horrified at the same time.

"Andrea," said Yakov, speaking to the gray-haired cop, "This man attacked me and Bekim." He pulled his hands away from his nose to reveal his bloody face. The officer looked at him, and then stared at Bekim, who was sitting with his back to a wall.

"Are you getting slow, Bekim?" said Andrea, apparently without much sympathy. He turned to me. "Is this true?"

I leaned and whispered in Leyla's ear, and she stepped away from me.

"Is what true?" I asked. I was already starting to feel guilty for letting my temper get the best of me, but until now, it hadn't occurred to me that I might get into *legal* trouble for brawling with a pimp and his bodyguard. In America, the cops would likely have pretended that Yakov had fallen down and hurt himself, and maybe even given me a pat on the back. However, here and now, the situation was different. I had assaulted a businessman in his place of work. I wasn't sure how to approach things, but I wanted Leyla to get away before they realized she was involved in any of this business.

"Did you attack these men?"

"Did I attack them?" All three policemen were focused on me as I parroted back the questions. Leyla edged toward the door.

"Stop repeating the question," said Andrea. "Answer me!"

Leyla was out into the hallway. I took a breath. "I'm not sure I should answer anything. I don't know how your legal system works."

Andrea tilted his head, as if he could see me better that way. "Are you refusing to answer my questions?"

"Well," I said, "only until I know more about what I should do."

"Andrea," barked Yakov, and made a curt gesture toward me.

The policeman did not looked pleased, but he nodded, and issued orders in Greek to his two companions. They each grabbed one of my arms, pulled them behind my back, and snapped handcuffs around my wrists.

"You will find out about our legal system, now," said Andrea.

THIRTEEN

I had been in jail a number of times in America to visit people, and also once before as an inmate. Prisoners were usually taken to a booking station where they got all your information, took all your stuff, and had you sign to agree that what they had taken from you was all that you had on you when you were arrested. They also took your clothes and gave you a pajama-like uniform, and then escorted you to a cell.

That wasn't quite how it went for me in Corfu.

I was driven to a large, ugly, depressing block building surrounded by chain link topped with barbed wire; the parking lot was full of police vehicles. Andrea and his cohorts escorted me past a reception station. They did a quick search, taking about fifty Euros from my pockets, as well as the hotel key and a bus pass. I wasn't carrying a wallet, and of course I didn't have my passport. I wondered how my lack of identification was going to go over when they booked me.

But if they booked me, I wasn't aware of it. After the search, they took me through two security doors, down a long hallway, and then to a small cell that appeared to be all by itself in that area of the building. It would have been considered old-fashioned in most of America, with actual steel bars forming the wall with the hallway and concrete block for the other three walls. There was a double bunk attached to each of the block walls, and in one corner, a stainless steel toilet-and-sink combination unit. It wasn't any too clean, and it smelled, but I was grateful to find that it was empty. My handcuffs were removed, the door unlocked, and I was shoved roughly into the room.

"Don't I get a phone call?" I asked. No one said anything, and the three officers walked away.

I sat down on one of the bunks, thought about things like fleas and bed-bugs, and stood up again. I went and stuck my hands through the bars, leaning on one of the cross-pieces, like someone in an old Western movie. It was something to cross off my bucket-list.

I was pretty sure Leyla had gotten clean away. Certainly, she hadn't done anything wrong, and there was no reason they should hold her, anyway, but I felt better knowing that she had gotten out of the house. She'd probably call Alex Chan, and sooner or later, someone would come looking for me.

I kept leaning, but it's tiresome looking cool when there's no one there to admire you for it. I wished I had an iPod or something. I ran through a Bach piece in my head, and then the 1812 overture by Tchaikovsky. Since I was in Greece, I tried to play some of the songs from the musical *Grease* in my head, but I couldn't make myself go through with it. Eventually, I settled for some old Elton John tunes and then some numbers by Mumford & Sons. I finally pushed myself off the bars, and began doing some Tae Kwon Do forms in the small open space of the cell. I began to breathe deeply and sweat a little, and it felt good.

Just as I was considering risking the bed-bugs again, I heard the door at the end of the hallway open up. Two of the cops who had locked me up were hustling several other men down the hallway to my cell. The guards opened the door and the prisoners pushed into my cell in a mass, not waiting in line. It looked like maybe six or eight men.

"Hey," I said to the cops. Andrea wasn't here, and I didn't know if they spoke English. I'd been considering what I might say if I saw anyone again. "Did you know I am a priest?"

They didn't say anything.

It was a bit of a gamble. I didn't know much about Greek culture, but it was possible that clergymen were still respected. I certainly don't think of myself as different from any other person, and I have never thought I was entitled to special treatment just because I was a clergyman, but at that point, I decided I'd take any advantage I could get. On the other hand, perhaps priests were an especially hated class of people.

"Eh-go eh-me episkopos," I said. In ancient Greek it meant, "I am a bishop." I had no idea if it meant anything to Modern Greek speakers. I couldn't remember the word for *priest*, and if they understood at all, *bishop* was probably close enough. They looked at me with sudden interest. One of them fired off a staccato burst of Greek at me, while the other locked the cell door. I shrugged helplessly, and pointed at myself. "Priest. Episkopos. I would like to make a phone call. I never got to make one."

The two officers looked at each other. One of them said something to the prisoners who had just entered my cell. Then they shrugged and left.

I turned to look at my new cell-mates. They all wore prison uniforms, and it made me feel a little left out. I bet that they had been properly booked, too. One of them stepped toward me, close enough to be provocative, and began eying me with a deliberate and insulting stare. He was lean and wiry and a little bit shorter than me. His eyes were small, and he looked mean and ready for trouble. He said something I didn't understand.

"That's the thing," I said to him. "I'm sure you just said something either insulting or scary. But with this language barrier, it all goes to waste."

"Priest?" said a voice from among the men. "Priest Borden? Is that you?" An athletic-looking young man with short, dark hair shouldered his way through the others and stood in front of me. It was Zef.

"Zef!" I said, surprised. "I guess now I know why we couldn't find you."

He waved his hand. "It is some mix up. In Albania, maybe I should go to jail, except we pay the police there, and they are a little afraid of me. But here, I have done nothing wrong. They think I am someone else."

I visit the jail in Grand Lake from time to time, and it's unusual to find an inmate who admits to doing anything wrong. I guess some things are the same the world over.

Zef opened his mouth again as if to say more, but he was interrupted by the mean, wiry man, who said something in either Greek or Albanian. Zef turned and spoke to him. Two others spoke up angrily, and there was a murmur of what sounded like agreement. Zef said something more, putting his hand palm out in the universal sign for "wait," and turned back to me.

"The Albanian Mafia has many connections in jails and prisons. We received a message that there is someone here who has displeased them. We are supposed to give this person a beating, and we are told that it will not matter if he dies. They will make sure we don't get into too much trouble."

I had heard about such things, of course. It happened in American prisons too.

"Zef, I know what you do for a living. But I can't stand by and watch it happen. I almost like you, but I can't let you do this." I looked at the other prisoners. "Which one is he?"

Zef looked at me steadily and without expression for a surprisingly long time. I was puzzled at first, until finally, it clicked.

"Oh," I said.

"Yes."

"I'm surprised," I said. "I thought you didn't work for those people."

"I have told you I work for the Albanian Mafia."

"No, I mean the human-trafficking part of it. You said you were just involved with the gambling part."

"That is true, but it is all connected. In any case, what does human trafficking have to do with this?"

"The man I have angered is the man who took Lena. Now, he has Talia also. His name is Yakov."

Zef's face darkened, and his lips drew a thin, taut line. "Tell me."

Just then, the mean guy spoke angrily, affirmed by several other voices.

Zef turned and snapped at them, his own voice matching their anger. He looked back at me.

I started to tell him about how the fake Lena had contacted us, but the men behind Zef interrupted again, raising their voices in hostility. Zef spoke to them again, this time more calmly, but they didn't seem to settle down. There were six men in addition to Zef, and they all drew around us in a threatening semi-circle.

Zef met my eyes and sighed. "It looks like we will have to fight, after all," he said.

My heart sank. I doubted I could have handled six men at one time, though there was always a faint hope. But Zef alone might prove to be too much for me. With him in the mix, there was only one way this was going to end.

"I am not afraid to die," I told him. "But it would be a terrible thing for my wife, Leyla. If you promise you won't let them kill me, I will not fight back. But if you will not promise, I will fight, and *I* promise *you*, some of them will be hurt very badly, maybe even you. You have seen a little bit of what I can do."

Zef looked at me in surprise. "No, no," he said. "I mean you and I together will have to fight them. Then you can tell me about Yakov and Lena."

For some reason, I felt slightly embarrassed. "Oh. Okay." I looked at the group, counting them again. "Do you think you can take three of them?"

He was looking at them too. "I think so," he said. "What about you? I could perhaps take one more if you cannot."

"No, I think it will be fine," I said. "How about the first one finished with his three helps the other one?"

"Good," he said, and promptly used his elbow to break the jaw of the man standing closest to him.

I suppose it was pandemonium for a while, but as always when I fight, time seemed to slow way down. It was like I could see what other people were going to do before they even began to do it. We had the advantage of surprise, since we had started the fight, and also since Zef was fighting on my side. Altogether, it was less than three minutes before all six men were in various positions on the floor, making diverse noises to indicate pain.

I felt a little queasy from a well-placed blow to my midsection, and I could taste blood and feel my lower lip swelling up. Zef had a bruise on his cheek that was rapidly swelling into a magnificent mouse, and he was gingerly poking at his ribs. I knew my knuckles would soon swell and ache from the blows I had delivered, and I assumed that the same would be true for Zef, also.

"Okay?" I asked.

He nodded.

"Just so you know," I said, "I helped you on that last one."

Zef was shaking his head. "It was not necessary. He was already going down."

"He might have been going for your legs."

He shook his head again. "I do not think so. But did you see me distract that other one for you, when you kicked the tall Greek?"

"How should I know which one is Greek and which one is Albanian?" I asked.

"When you strike them, they cry out in their native language."

It was probably the best set up line I would ever have. "It's all Greek to me," I said happily.

Zef frowned. "Albanian does not sound like Greek."

There was a slight pause while he looked at me. I sighed. "Never mind," I said. "So now what?"

Zef spoke loudly to those men who were still able to listen and process. Slowly, they crawled and hobbled to the other side of the cell. He gestured to a bunk, and we sat, Zef carefully holding a hand to his rib cage. "Now," he said, "Tell me about this Yakov."

"Do you know him?" I asked.

He shrugged. "Describe him to me."

When I told him about the scar on Yakov's face, Zef went very still, and his eyes went very bleak.

"I know him," he said.

FOURTEEN

No guards appeared until lights out. The two who came down the hallway were different than the cops who had brought me to the cell. When they saw the bruises and drying blood, there was a flurry of shouting and activity, and we were all made to stand with our hands on the wall above our heads and our feet apart. Three of the six men that Zef and I had fought were unable to do so. Zef grunted in pain as he put his hands above him on the bars of the cell.

"Ribs?" I asked.

He nodded.

Once the guards felt we were appropriately controlled, they called for backup. Four more guards appeared, and then two medical orderlies wheeling a cart with a bed on it. One by one, all of the men were taken to the infirmary. Though the orderlies kept coming back for more patients, none of the prisoners returned to the cell. With less visible damage than anyone else, I was finally alone again. I hoped Zef would get some help for his ribs.

Eventually, a guard and an orderly returned for me. I could feel a little bruising around my mouth and some random aches and pains, but it was my knuckles that hurt worst of all. Though I was initially going to refuse treatment, I decided to go along and see if I could get some ice.

They walked me down the hallway, and we took two right hand turns into a small infirmary. There were three beds in the room, and two of them were occupied by men who may or may not have been among my attackers. A man in a white coat with thick, curly grey hair approached me.

"They tell me you are an American," he said. His English was quite good.

"I am. Does it make a difference in my treatment?"

He didn't laugh. "Of course not," he said. "I am a doctor. I treat everyone as needed. But tell me, where are you hurt?"

I pointed to the corner of my mouth. "Here, of course," I said. I could feel blood flowing again, now that I had started talking. "Mostly, I just need ice for that, and for my hands."

He made me sit on the edge of the empty bed while he peered at my mouth. After that, he gingerly examined my hands, and then straightened up.

"I will give you ice for your hands. But your lip must be stitched."

"Really?" I asked in surprise. With the word, I could feel more blood flow again.

"Please do not talk anymore," he said. "It will be easier to suture if it is not bleeding so much." He went to a desk that stood in the corner, and then returned holding a mirror. "Regard," he said, putting it in front of my face. Sure enough, there was a gaping gash in my lower lip, extending to about half an inch past the edge of my mouth.

"Rats," I exclaimed. "This is really no good."

"It will be fine," said the doctor in a soothing voice. "I will make very small, neat sutures. It will heal well."

"Thank you," I said. But I was thinking it was a rotten thing, on your honeymoon, to be unable to kiss your wife.

FIFTEEN

After the sort of night that will never be described in a tour guide of Corfu, a guard came to fetch me in the morning. He led me back out to the front of the building, while I scratched suspiciously at myself, thinking of bed bugs and fleas. He took me into a reception area, and there was Leyla, standing with two other people.

"Jonah, your face!" said Leyla, and then hugged me fiercely.

"Sorry," I mumbled.

We broke apart and she looked at me. My guard was talking to the other people. He handed them something, then turned and left.

After holding Leyla again for a moment, I turned to the two newcomers. One was a man in his fifties with thick white hair and a tan face. His companion was a small, dark haired, olive-complexioned woman in her thirties.

"Joe Williams," said the man, sticking out his hand. I shook it, and approved of his firm grip. "I think perhaps you know Ms. Bianco," he added, nodding at the woman.

I looked closely at her. "Jasmine?" I said. She smiled, and then stepped forward and hugged me tightly. I noticed over her shoulder that Leyla had a kind of skeptical look on her face. We knew Jasmine from a few years back, and our association with her had been complicated, to say the least.

"What's going on?" I asked. "Why are you here?"

"It's a long story," she said, "And this is possibly the ugliest place in Corfu. Why don't we go get some coffee and we'll fill you in?"

"An excellent suggestion." I took Leyla's hand. "They let me keep my clothes," I said. "But I had a hotel key and about fifty Euros."

"They gave me the key," said Williams. "I doubt it's worth trying to get the fifty Euros back."

"And *I* might not let you keep those clothes," said Leyla, wrinkling her nose. "You are a little pungent right now."

"We can sit in the fresh air at a table in the street," I said. "But I think the coffee is more important than my wardrobe."

There are more sidewalk cafes in Corfu than fleas on a dog, or a prison cot, for that matter. It wasn't long before we were settled a table drinking the beverage that was called coffee by the godless Greeks.

I looked at Williams and Jasmine. "So, why am I free, and why are you two here? I'm guessing it's connected."

"I'm an attaché with the American embassy in Athens," said Williams. "Your attorney, Alex Chan, contacted us. We were working with the authorities to straighten out your passport situation when Ms. Bianco showed up."

Jasmine smiled. "I met Alex during that business on Lake Superior," she said to me. "We've sort of kept in touch. He knew I was in Europe, so when Leyla told him you were in jail, he reached out to me, also."

"Between us, we've managed to get the charges against you dropped," said Williams. "The Greek authorities want you to stay up in Paleokastritsa until we get your passport situation squared away, and then you'll go home."

"Thank you," I said. "There are worse places to be confined."

"You got that right." He slid a thin briefcase onto the table and opened the latches with two very satisfying clicks. The sleek case, and the way he opened it, made me think of a spy movie.

"What have you got for me this time, Q?" I asked. "A pen that turns into a missile? An aspirin tablet that turns into a boat?"

Everyone ignored me, especially Leyla.

Williams pulled out a small, cheap cell phone. It didn't go with the case at all.

"Rats," I said. Everyone continued to ignore me.

He handed me the phone. "Keep this with you at all times. The Greek authorities are requiring that we be able to reach you, day or night. That's a condition of your release. There's a GPS tracker on this thing, so we can confirm your whereabouts."

"Okay," I said, taking the phone. "Thank you again." Williams handed me a charger and a cord. I turned to Jasmine. "So what are you doing in Europe?"

"I'm on a joint task force we have with Interpol. I can't say very much about it."

"Of course not," I said. "I bet *you* get cool spy stuff, and not just a crummy, cheap cell phone."

"He said it has GPS," she said mildly.

"Can you even say what the task force is about?"

She smiled and shook her head.

I got a funny tickle on the back of my neck. "Is it about human trafficking?" I asked.

The smile faded. "How did you know that?"

"Lucky guess."

Jasmine was serious. "That's right. I forgot about your intuition thing." She glanced at Williams. "No one is supposed to know. This can't go beyond this table."

He nodded gravely. "I've kept a secret or two in my time. You're fine."

Jasmine turned back to Leyla and me. "What are you guys into? I know you were in the can for busting up a legal brothel. Is that why you thought I was in trafficking?"

We sketched the general picture of the situation with Talia, Lena, and Zef. "Let's just say, I'm not surprised Yakov dropped the charges," I said. "He probably doesn't want the police sniffing around him very much. I'm pretty sure that he's relevant to your task force."

Jasmine was already shaking her head. "I looked into your brothel-owner as soon as Alex told me about your situation. We kind of like to keep tabs on the legal ones, since they are already in the flesh business, and it might be tempting for them to get cheap, captive labor. Your guy has some minor connections to the Albanian mob, but he's small time. We're after the big fish."

"Well, he practically told me that he had taken two Albanian girls."

"And you beat him up," said Williams. "And he dropped charges against you. No offense, but I'm not sure your testimony about what he may or may not have said to you during a highly dubious incident is going to help Ms. Bianco's task force very much."

"Are you calling me a liar?" I asked, feeling a little hot in the face. Leyla put her hand on my arm.

"Not at all," said Williams calmly. "I'm just playing out how a discussion might go in an Interpol conference room or a courtroom."

"Joe is right," said Jasmine. "I believe you, but that doesn't bring us any closer to getting the scumbag for human trafficking. And like I said, we're after the big fish here. It's an *international* task force. Our respective governments are not going to be impressed if we go around busting up small-time legal pimps because tourists suspect that they use an illegal girl once in a while. I understand that it's a tragedy for those two Albanian girls, but we're after a major trafficking ring that is moving large numbers of girls from Eastern Europe, North Africa, and the Middle East." She shrugged. "I'm sorry, but it comes down to politics. Your guy is small time and probably mostly legal. Just be thankful he isn't pressing charges."

"Probably the girls working for him don't feel like it's small time," I said, my voice sounded thick and angry, even to me. "It's probably a pretty big deal in their lives."

She looked from Leyla to me, sympathetically. "Look, this is a nasty business. I'm here because I hate it, and I want to stop it. But you can't just come into a foreign country and tell them their laws are wrong and beat up anyone who disagrees with you." She smiled and winked. "Don't get me wrong, I'm glad you roughed this guy up, and I wish he'd go out of business. But we can't win all the battles. For now, we're going after the big fish. Your guy may pick up an illegal here and there, but the way to help the biggest number of girls is to stop it at the source."

"What about our friend, Talia?" asked Leyla.

Jasmine looked grim. "We'll do what we can, but the main effort has to be spent on getting the big guys. In the end, we'll save a lot more girls that way than by just going after a guy who brings one or two illegals in to work his brothel in Greece."

"So we're on our own."

Joe Williams put his palm firmly on the middle of the table and made sure both Leyla and I made eye contact with him. "No, you are not on your own. What you *are,* is completely out of it. I did some checking of my own, Borden, and I heard you have a tendency to go on a crusade once in a while. You will not do that here in Greece, not on my watch. You will go back to your hotel, enjoy your vacation and when we get your passport mess straightened out, you will go home and raise awareness about human trafficking. But here, now, you do nothing." He kept his hand in the middle of the table, dominating the group with body language. "Understand?"

"I don't like it."

"I hate it," said Leyla.

Williams nodded. "Good kids. You *should* hate it. But you're going to get with the program anyway, right?"

I wondered if Williams had been a drill instructor in his youth. Finally, I nodded. Leyla said, "Fine." Williams removed his hand.

I looked at Jasmine. "One way or another, we saved each other's lives back on Superior, didn't we?"

She looked uncomfortable. "Jonah, there's nothing I can do for you here. Joe is from the embassy, and he's got the final say on the situation with you two while you're in Greece. It isn't my jurisdiction." She glanced at him. "And it so happens that he is right."

"So, get your big fish," said Leyla. "That is your job. But maybe, can you spare enough time and energy to look into the situation with our friend, Talia? That wouldn't be so far outside your job, would it?"

She nodded and sighed. "I can't make promises, but I'll see what I can do."

"You might start with this guy, Zef," I said. "He isn't in human trafficking, but he has ties to the Albanian mob. He might even help you with your big fish."

"Thanks," said Jasmine. "I'll look into it."

"He's actually not a bad guy," I said. "I mean, I know he's technically a mob enforcer, but I think he's got a good heart."

Jasmine stared at me for a long time. "You haven't changed a bit, have you? You are still a piece of work."

"Thanks for noticing," I said.

SIXTEEN

"Well, the good news is, we get to enjoy our honeymoon again," said Leyla. It was evening, and we were walking up the road to the little convent of the cats on top of the cliffs near our hotel. The plan was to watch the sun as it went down somewhere near Italy, and to take far too many photographs of the event.

I looked at the beautiful bay below us. "Yes, if we are going to be confined somewhere, this is the place to be."

We reached the top of the hill and crossed to the seaward side where the convent sprawled peacefully in the late, golden sunlight, looking out over the Ionian Sea west toward Italy. Taking the small flagstone path into the grounds, we strolled around until we found a vantage point overlooking the ocean. There was a big pine tree to our left and flowers in pots all around. As we leaned on the waist-high stone wall, a calico cat stalked up to us, and began rubbing on our legs. I reached down to scratch its ears.

Leyla began taking pictures with her camera. I heard giggling to the right, and turned to see three young women standing in a doorway that led back into the dim recesses of the complex. They might have been the nuns we had seen a few days ago, but if so, they were out of uniform. Leyla turned also, and I could hear the camera clicking as she took several pictures.

"Perfect!" she murmured. "Candid nuns, relaxing in street clothes at the end of the day."

As soon as the girls realized Leyla had a camera, they quit talking and withdrew quickly.

"I got some great shots," said Leyla. "Those are going to be pretty unique pictures."

We turned back to the sunset, and the camera whirred some more. At last, Leyla let it hang from her neck, and I put my arm around her as we leaned against the wall to drink in the view.

"May I help you?"

I turned again, and there was the young, athletic-looking priest with the expensive haircut and neatly trimmed beard. His dark eyes were somehow very intense. That odd thought twitched in the back of my head again, but I still couldn't quite make it surface. I assumed it was probably just dislike from our first meeting.

Leyla forced a smile at him. "Just taking pictures of the sunset," she said, sweeping her arm out to encompass the beautiful view in front of us.

"Would you like me to take a picture of the two together?" He asked. Apparently, he was offering us an olive leaf. Either that, or he didn't recognize us from our first meeting where he had insulted us and I had hit him.

"You are Greek?" asked Leyla, apparently curious about his accent.

"Of course," said the priest, nodding. "I am part of the convent here." He held out his hand for the camera, and Leyla gave it to him.

We stood against the wall near the pine tree. "Try to get the ocean, and the pine and sunset too," said Leyla.

"You don't want much," I murmured, and she elbowed me in the side as she snuggled up under my arm for the picture.

The priest seemed to be taking a long time, looking at the camera with a frown on his face.

"We're ready," said Leyla loudly, to get his attention. "You just point it, and hold that button down gently, and then press it all the way."

"Of course," said the priest. "I am sorry." He slowly lifted the camera, fiddling with it some more as he did. At last, he took the picture.

Leyla reached for the camera, and he seemed reluctant to hand it back. "I am not sure if it is good," he said.

"Let's take a look," said Leyla, still holding her hand out.

My mind was still furiously trying to uncover that little thing that was bothering me. I watched the priest as he slowly passed the camera to Leyla. He was such a contrast to the other Orthodox priests we had seen, who were generally wild haired and bushy-bearded.

"Falamendjerit," I said absent-mindedly as he put the camera in Leyla's hand. Suddenly, it clicked. This man was neatly trimmed, but Orthodox priests are not allowed to trim their hair and beards.

"Ska-jyuh," replied the priest, nodding his head.

"No, Jonah," Leyla was saying, "Falamendjerit is Albanian, and he said he was..." she trailed off as she realized he had given the typical Albanian response.

"You're not Greek?" she asked him. "You are Albanian?"

"He's not a priest, either," I said.

"I really wish you had not taken pictures of those girls, and said these things," said the priest, and from somewhere among his robes, he produced a large automatic pistol and pointed it at us.

SEVENTEEN

We both stared at him.

"What are you doing?" I asked at last.

"Please give me the camera," he said, nodding to Leyla.

She looked down at it and suddenly her expression changed. She hurled the camera over the wall. It sailed toward the sunset, past the edge of the cliff and plummeted beyond our line vision, presumably ending up in the ocean, almost two hundred feet below.

The priest's face darkened in anger. "Why did you do this foolish thing?"

"I don't like it when people point guns at me," said Leyla angrily. "Put that away. We're going now."

She started to move, and I also took a step, but the priest shifted to block our path and thumbed back the hammer on his pistol with a loud click. We both stopped.

"I cannot let you leave. I think you know too much."

"Well, *now* we do," I said. "And that is your fault. All I knew two seconds ago is that you weren't a priest and you weren't Greek." I paused for effect, hoping my ploy would convince him. "Now, we also know that you are a thief, who holds up tourists at gunpoint."

Leyla glanced quickly at me, and then looked back at him and nodded. "Yes. But I threw away the camera, to show you that crime doesn't pay, and we have no money with us. We are leaving." She started to move again, but he lifted the gun. I could see him struggling with it. At last, he shook his head.

"No. It is too risky. You must come with me." He gestured with his other hand. Reluctantly, we started walking where he directed.

He brought us into a long, sunken courtyard, cool and covered by vine branches. It felt almost like a tunnel. Halfway along, he gestured, and we turned left, passing through a thick stone doorway. I slowed down, looking at the large stones with interest and bending slightly to examine the smooth flagstone floor. The times we had come up to the convent in the past, this area had been closed off to tourists.

"This is awesome!" I said. "This place must be hundreds of years old."

"Keep moving," said the priest behind us, his voice sharp with tension. "This is not a tour."

"But can we see the chapel?" I asked.

No one seemed to think it was as funny as I did. Maybe I didn't think it was funny either, and it was just a way to take my mind off our situation. But part of me thought that maybe I really did think it was funny. Maybe I needed to get out more.

We kept moving down the long narrow stone-paved hallway. We turned right and came to a descending flight of steps. There was a landing a short way down where the steps turned a corner. I began to breathe deeply and consciously loosen my muscles. This might be a good place to catch him off-guard.

"Stop."

The priest moved up to me, grabbing the back of my shirt and shoving the gun into my lower back. He nodded at Leyla. "We will go slow and careful."

I tried not to let my disappointment show and stepped slowly, awkwardly, down the stairs after Leyla, while the man behind me held my shirt.

We emerged into another hallway, this one much darker. The priest kept his gun in contact with my back and marched us past several doors on both sides. The hall intersected with another one coming in from the left, and he moved us in that direction. This next corridor was brightly lit by a window at the end, and I caught a glimpse of the sea and the sunset. Just before we reached the end, the priest stopped and opened the door on the right, gesturing us into a room.

This room was even brighter than the hallway outside. It faced almost directly west, and two windows with thick sills admitted the golden light of the setting sun. It was a large space holding a long, rough dining table with matching chairs, as well as several comfortable-looking upholstered seats and two couches. The room also held about fifty young women who stopped talking as we entered. A lot of them looked as young as thirteen or fourteen. None of them looked older than twenty-five.

The priest entered the room behind us, still holding his gun in plain sight. He spoke out loudly in English. "We have a situation that we must take care of. You will all stay in this room. We will bring your food soon."

He looked as if he enjoyed the attention the girls were paying him, as if he liked it that they thought he was dangerous and important. He turned and stepped outside the door, shutting it. There was a brief rattle as he locked it. I quickly swept the room with my eyes and noticed another door, presumably entering the same hallway. Before I could move to it, it too rattled as it was locked from the outside. Just to be sure, I checked both doors, but they were indeed locked.

"The windows!" said Leyla.

She rushed to the one on the right, while I took the one on the left. They were old-style, single pane with panels that swung out. Mine was already open to admit the breeze. My elation turned to bitterness, however, when I thrust my upper body across the thick sill to see outside. The room we were in was built into the side of the cliff. If we went out the windows, it would be a one-hundred and fifty foot fall to the jagged rocks below. I pulled my head back in and looked over at Leyla, whose expression matched my feelings. Suddenly, her face changed."

"Jonah! Your phone!"

"Of course!" I said. I whipped it out of my pocket. Joe Williams had programmed his number into it. I found it and hit the send button. Nothing happened. I pulled the phone away from my face, and realized that there was no reception.

"No service. I bet these stone walls are too thick, and we're partly underground as it is."

I walked quickly around the room and even tried to hang out the window a little, but I still couldn't get any service. At last, I gave up.

The young women in the room were regarding us with interest. A few of them had dark skin and the distinctive aquiline features of northeastern Africa; perhaps Ethiopia, or maybe Eritrea. Many others looked vaguely like the way I imagined Arabian women might look, but one rarely actually saw the faces of Arabian women, so I couldn't be sure. Maybe they were Lebanese or Syrian. A few were clearly Eastern European, and several others looked to me like Albanians, especially one particular girl, but maybe that was because she reminded me of Talia. They were all wearing ordinary clothes, and there was not a nun habit to be seen. A sudden thought struck me.

"Lena?" I said loudly. "Is there someone here named Lena?"

The particularly Albanian-looking girl stepped forward hesitantly. "Yes. I am called Lena. Please, what is happening?" I could see Leyla looking at me thoughtfully.

I took a step nearer. The girl called Lena had more than a passing resemblance to Talia.

"Do you have a cousin named Talia?" I asked.

"But, yes," she said. "How do you know this?"

EIGHTEEN

We explained as briefly as we could.

"We are in trouble," said Leyla in summary. "Very bad trouble. They will probably kill us. They will take all of you and make you into slaves. Sex-slaves."

Lena was shaking her head. "No, no. We have paid them to transport us to the European Union. I know this is not good for the law, but we will be good when we get there. We will be free. We have already paid these men to help us."

Lena's grasp of English was not quite as good as Talia's, but we were getting the gist of the meanings back and forth between us. "If it's all fine, then why did that man point a gun at us?" I said.

"Of course it is not good for the law," said Lena, waving her hand. "It is –" she searched for the English word.

"Illegal?" suggested Leyla.

"Yes. It is illegal for us to go to the EU this way. That is why this man points the gun and locks you in here. But when we are gone, he will let you go. I have been here one week now, while other girls come, and this man has not hurt us. He is not bad."

"If you are so sure, why don't you just walk out the door here? Greece is in the EU."

Lena snorted. "Greece is okay. Talia lives here, and it is okay. But it is still a poor country and still difficult to live here. Perhaps it will even lose EU status soon. And it is close to Albania, too easy to get caught and put back. It will be better for me in Italy or Austria. I have paid to go there, so I will not stop in Greece. You will see. Talia will see."

"We know Zef, also. He says you are making a mistake. He says these people are bad."

Lena's face changed. "Zef," she said, her contempt unmistakable. "He thinks he is a cowboy, with his silly boots and American jeans. He thinks he love me. He is only jealous."

"You don't love him?" asked Leyla.

She laughed. "He is handsome, and he was nice to me. But I do not love him. He just want me for himself, but I do not want him."

"I think you are making a mistake. We are worried that these men will enslave you once they have taken you where they want."

Lena waved a hand again. She seemed fond of the gesture. "No, it is fine. I will be good. You can tell Talia I am good."

"But we cannot find Talia. She is missing."

Lena looked troubled for a moment, but then her face cleared. "You are foreigners, you do not understand. She is not missing; you just do not know where to find her."

It began to occur to me that perhaps Lena was not terribly bright. I decided it wasn't worth trying to convince her that Talia was in danger.

"Do you have a phone, so Talia can call you?" I asked, changing tactics.

"No, they took our phones when we began. I'm very sorry for I couldn't call Talia, but it was necessary."

I looked over at Leyla, and then back at Lena. "I would like to give you a phone. If these people really mean you no harm, it will not hurt them for you to have it, and you do not need to tell them about it."

Leyla met my eyes. "Are you sure?"

"I think it might be best."

"But this is your phone!" said Lena.

I pulled it out of my pocket and showed it to her. "It isn't expensive. In fact, it didn't cost me anything at all. Really." I could see Lena wavering. "I can't even use this when I go back to America, so you might as well have it."

Slowly, she reached out her hand and took the phone.

"Keep it safe, keep it hidden. You can use it to call Talia after you are settled."

"Thank you."

Leyla took my arm and drew me aside. "Jonah, are you sure?" she asked in a low voice. "We might get reception and be able to call for help."

"I think this is for the best. We certainly don't have reception here, and maybe they are jamming cell signals in the entire complex. In any case, they are almost certain to search us when they come back, and then we'll lose the phone anyway. This way, maybe Lena has a chance somewhere down the road."

"Jonah, don't you give up on *us*."

"Not a chance, don't worry. I just don't think the phone is the answer."

"You really think they'll search us?"

"I would, if it were me."

Leyla turned back to Lena. "Do you have any hair pins or bands?"

Lena handed some things to Leyla. Since I keep my hair short, I had no idea what they were. Leyla bent over, allowing all her hair to fall forward. She reached up and did some things, and ended up with her hair in some sort of bun or something – in any case, it was all gathered up into one mass on her head. It was hastily done, but I admired how it set off her neck and profile, even while I was amazed that she could think of her hair at such a moment.

She squeezed my arm, and as we turned back to speak with Lena, there was a rattle at the door, and then it opened. Five men stepped through, including the young fake priest. I felt a small glow of pleasure that they thought I might have overwhelmed them if they had brought fewer. Immediately, I repented of my pride, thinking repentance was appropriate in a convent. I thought humbly that perhaps they had one man to cover Leyla, so only four were for me.

Regardless, that number, along with the priest's gun, was plenty, so when they searched us, we let them. Once more, my hotel key was taken from me. I wondered if I should get a fake rock to hide it under, the next time I left the room. When they were done searching us, Leyla looked at me and nodded ever so slightly. Just newlyweds, and already she was learning to admit when I had been right. Things were looking up.

The next part wasn't so fun. One of the men hustled Leyla away, out the door, and into the hallway, while two others held my arms and another stood by expectantly. The priest handed his gun to the free man and rolled his shoulders. Leyla called to me, and when I tried to step towards her, the man pointed the gun at my head, while the priest hit me in the solar plexus. He stepped back, and then did it again. No doubt, he felt he was entitled to some sort of payback for the first time we met.

I felt a little short of breath, and a little nauseous, but the worst part was the feeling of anger combined with helplessness.

"We take her away, and if you are nice, we do not harm her," said the priest, smugly. "If you are angry, or you try to escape, she will be hurt." He shrugged. "Maybe we kill her, maybe we sell her, I don't know."

I glared at him. He returned the look thoughtfully.

"Do you understand?"

I hated it, but I did understand. I nodded.

"You will..." he searched for the English word, "behave. Yes?"

"Yes."

He spoke to the men holding me. They let me go and stepped back, looking at me warily as if I was some sort of tiger out of its cage.

"We have heard from a friend that you can fight. But your wife, she cannot fight like you. Remember this."

I nodded again. "I get it. I won't attack you."

Satisfied, the priest nodded again and spoke to the other men. Still glancing at me, they turned and began to move among the young women in the room, who were standing in a group, staring at us. Lena gave me a short, but troubled look, and then turned away as the men led them out.

When they were gone, the priest led me back out of the room and down the sunlit hallway and then left at the T-junction with the darker corridor. There were doors spaced at regular, short intervals on both sides. He took some keys from inside his robe and opened a door on the left-hand side. Standing aside, he gestured me in. I paused in the doorway.

"What now?" I asked.

"Nothing," he said. "You wait. Remember, we have your wife." He gestured at the doorway again.

Reluctantly, I stepped inside, and he quickly shut the door behind me, locking it.

I found myself in a small room, maybe twelve feet by twelve. To my left was a bed. To my right was a small wardrobe and a washstand holding a bowl and a jug of water. Directly in front of me was a window with a thick sill. The floor was stone and the walls appeared to be stone also, solid and whitewashed. I was obviously in a monk's cell, or more precisely, in this case, a nun's.

I went to the window and found that it opened over the cliff overlooking the sea. The sun had passed beyond the rim of the sky and water, and a limpid twilight filled the air. The waves gently sighed as they washed the rocks below. We had been right to come out to see the sun set: it was a beautiful night.

Looking out the window, both up and down, I began to scope out handholds. I stretched out as far as I dared to see if the water at the base of the cliff was deep and free from rocks, but then I remembered what the priest had said about Leyla. As long as they had her, I wasn't going to try anything.

I laid down on the bed, leaving the window open, and tried to think things through. Obviously, we had stumbled onto the human-trafficking operation. For some reason, they were bringing the girls to Corfu disguised as nuns. Why they brought them all the way over to Paleokastritsa on the west coast, away from the main port at

Corfu Town, I couldn't imagine, nor what they did next. I wondered how they managed to use the convent without the Greek Orthodox Church knowing about it.

I also wondered how Yakov was involved. Was Jasmine right, and he was just a small-time legal pimp, albeit a very hateful one? True, Lena was here, and Yakov had said he now "owned" her, but maybe he was just yanking my chain. But why would he do that at all, and why pick on me? As I thought about it more, I realized I couldn't take Yakov out of the equation. After I started poking around looking for Talia and Lena, he had sent for me, twice, and he knew where Talia lived, and he knew about Lena. And since Lena was here in the convent, clearly Yakov was involved with a bigger operation than merely smuggling a few illegals out of Albania to work in his brothel.

Over the years, I've heard many people say that asking the questions is more important than finding the answers. In my considered, theological judgment, that's a bunch of horse-hooey. I wanted answers.

It was a beautiful night, but it began to pass very, very slowly. I stayed on the bed for a while. Then I got up and paced, four steps to the door, four back to the window. I tried to figure out how many laps I would have to do to walk a mile, but I was bored with the pacing long before I was finished. I looked at the jug and the washstand. I looked into the wardrobe and found it empty, except for a few wire hangers. I lounged on the bed. After a while, I went really wild and crazy, and poured some of the water from the jug into the washbowl and washed my face. I sat back on the bed, and tried to calculate the area of the room in cubits. A biblical cubit is about the length of a person's forearm from the elbow to the end of the fingers. The question was, whose forearm, exactly, mine, or that of a professional basketball player, or of a midget? It suddenly occurred to me to wonder if both of my forearms were the same length, and I spent seventeen happy seconds finding out.

Then, as I leaned on one of my cubits, a deliciously exciting idea occurred to me. I could take the dirty water in the washbasin, and throw it out the window. I decided to keep it as something to look forward to, and so I waited until I couldn't stand it any longer. At last I stood up, savoring the sensation of having something to do. The basin was white, made of enamel-coated metal. I examined it closely, and then lifted it carefully from the washstand with two hands, so as not to spill it. I walked all three steps to the open window, leaned out across the wide sill and transferred the basin to my left hand, holding it by the rim. I stuck my arm out the window and upended the basin. As the water sloshed out, the bowl slipped from my fingers, and fell with a small clattering sound.

I slid my head and shoulders out the window and looked down. The basin was resting on a ledge just a few feet down from my window. The ledge looked wide enough to stand on. Here was something more to do – I could retrieve the bowl. Without over-analyzing my motives, I scooched up into the wide window opening, and slid out, feet first. Holding the inside edge of the sill with my hands, I lowered myself until my feet touched the ledge where the basin was resting. Slowly and carefully, still holding on with my left hand inside the room, I bent my knees, and reached my right hand for the enamel bowl. My fingers groping for it touched the rim, and then as I sought a better grip on it, it wobbled and tumbled off the cliff into the empty air below me. It was too small to make a splash that was audible over the sound of the waves below.

I reached up with my right hand, grabbing the inside of the window, and pulled myself upright until I was standing on the ledge outside the window. There was a three-quarter moon, and in the clear air visibility was quite good. I looked at the cliff face above me and found I could see it in detail. It wasn't far to the top, and it was much like the rock face I had climbed in the bay, the one I had jumped off into the water to impress Leyla. It was rough and broken, filled with handholds for a casual climber.

I paused. I couldn't do anything while they held Leyla captive. But maybe, if I got loose, I could free Leyla.

Slowly, I started to climb.

NINETEEN

Although there were plenty of outcroppings for my hands and feet, they weren't all solid. The first one I grabbed with my right hand wiggled a little bit. I found another one further over that stayed put. After that, I tested each one carefully before transferring my weight to it. There really wasn't much difference between climbing here and climbing in the little bay as I had a few days before. The one main distinction was that here, I was about one hundred feet higher, and my chances of dying if I fell were much greater. I didn't look down, however, and the closeness of the top was encouraging. I took it slowly and carefully and tried to ignore the pounding of my heart and the adrenaline that rushed through my veins every time a foot or hand slipped.

The worst part came when I actually reached the top. My feet were spread out on two outcroppings when I reached up over the edge, and found only grass and dirt, sloped toward me. There was nothing to hang on to, and the slope meant that if I simply tried to heave myself up, I might just slide right back off.

I hung there for a long time, scrabbling with my right hand, and then my left. I had no place to go. At last, I realized I had to either go down, or work my way around until I found a firm place to get over the edge. Grabbing onto my previous handhold, I looked down for a new foothold below me and to the right. In the moonlight I could see the foaming waves breaking on sharp rocks, far, far below. For a moment, it felt like my whole world was spinning, I quickly looked up again, hugging the cliff until I could calm down. It took a long time to regain the courage to try again. This time, prepared for the view, I tried to concentrate on only looking at the cliff nearby, focusing on outcroppings, ledges, and cracks I might use. At last I found one, and slowly, carefully, transferred my right foot. Next came a new place for my right hand, and then my left hand, and finally my left foot.

It seemed like an eternity as I worked my way along the cliff. At last, I found a place where the edge looked a little more perpendicular. I reached my right hand up, and it closed around a tree root. I yanked on it, and it seemed firm. I took a step up with my right foot, and threw my left hand over the edge, finding another root. In a moment I was scrambling up and found myself holding onto the big pine tree that had framed our sunset picture a few hours before. It seemed to me like it had been months ago that we gave our camera to the priest for that picture. I crawled over until I was lying between the tree and the stone wall of the convent. There I caught my breath and waited for the shaking in my body to subside.

While I rested, I listened. Mostly, I heard the waves washing the rocks below me. I certainly didn't hear the sound of any people moving about near the wall.

At last, I stood up. The wall on this side was higher than the other. When we had our picture taken on the other side, we had leaned comfortably against the wall with our elbows resting on it. But from this side, it was over my head. I didn't relish the idea of jumping for it, missing, and losing my balance to go over the cliff. Instead, I found that the pine tree was close enough so that I could push against it with my feet while I walked my hands up the wall.

Even so, when my fingers closed on the top of the wall, I was going over blind. Anyone or anything could be waiting for me, and I had probably made enough noise with my scrambling to alert any guards. I paused, and then figured it was time to fish, or cut bait. I heaved myself on top of the parapet and found myself staring into a pair of very interested eyes.

TWENTY

They were wide, round eyes, and they belonged to a large tabby tomcat who had leaped onto the balustrade at the same moment I had heaved myself up. He slowly reached out a paw with claws retracted and tapped my arm, as if to make sure what he was seeing was really there.

"Hey, buddy," I said softly. "I'm sure glad it was you and not someone else." I wondered briefly if the cat understood me, and then laughed at myself. Of course he couldn't – he probably only spoke Greek.

That made me wonder if I was going a little crazy, but I finally decided it was unlikely, seeing as I had already done that, years ago.

I slid my legs over the wall and then crouched, so that I wouldn't be silhouetted against the lighter sea and sky. Glancing around, the convent looked deserted, except for the tomcat. A moment later, I amended my assessment, as another, smaller cat walked boldly from behind a bush and began rubbing itself against my knee. The tomcat above me on the wall, still interested, patted the top of my head with a gentle paw.

"Well, better this than watchdogs," I told them.

I reached out to pet the smaller cat, which began purring loudly. While I stroked it, I tried to think. The logical thing to do was get out of the convent, get down the hill, and call the police. But I wasn't so sure. My last encounter with the police wasn't exactly bursting with positivity. Obviously, someone in the jail had assisted Yakov by moving Zef and the other men into my cell to hurt me. Zef himself had told us that at least some officers were corrupted, and I had no way to know which ones. I could contact Joe Williams or Jasmine, except for the fact that their numbers were stored in the phone I had given Lena; I hadn't written them down. I wondered if anyone ever wrote down a phone number anymore.

No, my only good option was to try to free Leyla, and get away with her. Once we were safely gone, we could consider the next move.

Still not wanting to show a silhouette, I crawled away from the wall, feeling slightly foolish as the smaller cat came along with me, continuing to rub against me and purr as I tried to sneak along. I came to a set of descending stone steps, and as soon as I was well below the level of the surrounding grounds, I straightened up. I was in the sunken walkway, and it was significantly darker here in the shade of the vines. Ahead of me, a soft light was spilling from an arched doorway.

It was the same door we had come through earlier. Stepping very carefully, I crept through the entry way. The light was coming from another doorway down the corridor to the left, though there was no sound. Slowly I moved in that direction, not really sure what I might find, but thinking I needed to discover where they kept keys to the rooms in the convent. The room I found was some sort of library, and it was empty of people. There was a large, shabby rug covering most of the stone floor, and three walls were lined with book cases. A long, old fashioned couch with tall wooden legs was against the wall just to the left of the door, and several big armchairs were scattered around the room. A reading lamp was on, next to one of the armchairs, and an open book lay face-down on the chair. I went over and picked up the book. It was in Greek, but it looked like some sort of children's fairy-tale compendium, with large print and lots of colored pictures.

I heard a noise from the hall. Looking wildly around, I could see that the only way in or out of the library was through the one door that I had used. Since the noise was in the hall, it would be suicide to go out. I took the only remaining choice and threw myself flat onto the floor, scooting underneath the couch.

Footsteps shuffled slowly closer, and then I saw a pair of large feet, clad in sandals, coming through the door. The owner of the feet seemed to shamble more than step, and moved very slowly. I heard a low mumbling, and realized that the man who had entered was muttering to himself.

The feet shuffled over to the chair with the book, and the owner sat down, the chair cushions squeaking in protest. From my place under the couch, I was partly behind, and partly to one side, of the man in the chair. He was clearly a very tall individual, with a wild unruly mop of reddish-brown hair and a thick, unkempt beard of the same color. He wore the dark robes of an Orthodox priest. Something about him seemed very familiar.

He picked up the fairy tale book and as he looked at it, he began moving his lips slowly. Spittle collected around his mouth, sprayed into the air around him, and settled into his wild beard. As I watched him, something clicked. He had been on the ferry ride back from our aborted trip to Albania. I had seen him in the company of the young, fake-priest who had taken us hostage.

I remembered seeing his lips move while he read a book on the ferry. At the time, I had wondered if he was reading in a foreign language. Now, however, I knew he was reading in Greek, and a children's book at that. This time, I could observe him closely without any social awkwardness, and it seemed to me that perhaps there was something wrong with him. If I had to guess, I would have said that, technically, he was a few sandwiches short of a picnic.

Hiding under a couch while watching a mentally disabled Greek priest read children's stories has its undeniable attractions. For one thing, it was about seven times more exciting than anything I had found to do in my nun's cell. Even so, after a while, I began to feel that I might be able to utilize my time more effectively in other ways. I was just wondering if he was out of it enough for me to sneak out right past him, when I head firm steps coming down the hallway.

A pair of shiny black leather shoes appeared in front of me, and then I heard the voice of the young, urbane, fake priest. Unfortunately, he wasn't speaking English. Darn foreigners.

At first, the large, wild priest did not respond. The fake-priest spoke again, and then I could see the wild one look up from his book. One of his eyes seemed a little off from the other. He responded with a thick mumble, which sprayed more spittle into the air and into his beard. As I watched him and listened to him, I grew more convinced than ever that there was something wrong with him. He looked and sounded a little like some of the stroke victims I had visited during the course of my ministry back in Grand Lake.

The young priest said something else, and the disabled one responded again, slowly and thickly. He arose, and I could see that he carried his left arm awkwardly, again giving me the impression of a stroke victim. The younger one walked over to the chair and handed the taller priest a little cup. I couldn't tell, but it looked like there was a pill in it. The disabled man tipped the cup back to his mouth, and then took a glass of water which the younger man handed him, swallowing. A little bit of water dribbled down his beard. The fake-priest said something else, and then took the arm of his elder, escorting him from the room.

My mind raced. It might be best to follow them quickly. The older priest was probably no threat, and the younger one would be distracted by him as long as they were together, making it easier to follow them without detection. I had just started to slide out from my hiding place when footsteps sounded loudly outside the door. I froze, still underneath the couch. I could see the shiny shoes of the young priest as he stepped into the middle of the room, and then paused. For a wild moment, I thought I had been discovered, but then he moved over to the reading lamp, switched it off, and left the room again.

TWENTY-ONE

My pulse was still racing wildly from the fright that I had been discovered, but I realized that it was probably still a good idea to follow the priests. Maybe the young one would lead me to where Leyla was being held, or at least maybe following him would reveal where he kept the keys; *if* he was the one who kept the keys.

I slid out from under the couch and crawled to the doorway, slowly and carefully hitching my eyes around the edge at ground level. If anyone glanced back, they were more likely to notice a face looking at them from eye level. My chances of concealment were better if my face did not appear where they would naturally look.

Apparently, it would not have mattered either way. The two men were rounding a corner to my right, and they disappeared from view almost as soon as I saw them. I pulled my head back into the library and sat up, hastily removing my shoes and socks. Tying them together by the laces, I secured them to my belt and then ran quickly and silently down the hall in my socks to the corner where the priests had turned. I lay flat once more and carefully looked around the edge.

Another corridor ran off to my right. The fourth door down and across the hall from me stood ajar, with light spilling from a room into the hallway. I could hear voices, and it sounded like the two priests.

A woman in a nun's habit came up the corridor from the other direction. It was hard to tell in the dim light, but she looked older than the girls I had been seeing in habits lately, and she moved differently as well. In short, she looked more to me like a typical nun should look. She turned into the same room as the priests, and I heard a female voice join the conversation.

Before I had time to reflect on her presence, the young priest, the fake one, came back out of the room and started down the corridor toward where I lay. I slid my head back out of his sight and, as quickly and quietly as I could, scrambled to my feet. I threw a short glance over my shoulder. The library was too far, I would never make it back there before he came around the corner. There were a few other doors closer at hand, but I had no way of knowing if they were locked or not. I berated myself for not considering this possibility. There was only one thing to do, and anyway, he had threatened Leyla.

I stood flat against the wall just around the corner from the approaching man. When he reached the corner and started around, I brought my left fist all the way around in a half circle, using the momentum of my whole body to smash it into the point where his jaw met his neck. It's harder than most people realize to knock a man unconscious, but there is a pretty reliable trigger point just there, which often shuts off the lights immediately. I must have hit it just right. The left side of the priest's head, driven by my blow on his right, knocked against the wall, and then he slid to the ground in a heap. I doubt he ever saw it coming, and for a moment, I felt bad. Then, I remembered that he was involved in selling young girls into the sex trade. Once that popped into my head, I kind of wished I had hit him harder.

Most people who are rendered unconscious by a human fist don't stay out for very long, so I knelt immediately, searching through the man's robes for a set of keys. My hands encountered his gun, and I paused. I wanted to take it, and yet I was hopeful that perhaps the man, not knowing what hit him, would assume he had slipped and fallen on his own. If his gun was missing, he would know immediately that an enemy was on the loose, and would certainly call on his companions for help.

Too late, I heard the soft footstep. I looked up and saw the nun who had gone into the room with the two priests. She was standing in front of me, the door behind her still open and shedding light into the dim corridor. Once more, I was struck by the thought that this time, I was looking at the genuine article. She met my eyes, and then looked at the gun in my hand. Neither of us said anything for a moment.

Suddenly, she gestured at the gun and let loose a burst of speech that I thought was probably Greek. It sounded like a question.

I shrugged, coming to a decision. "I'm sorry. It's ridiculous, I know, but I only speak English." I ejected the shell in the firing chamber of the gun, and then pulled out the magazine, thumbing all the bullets out of it, and putting them in my pocket.

The nun spoke again. I shrugged again and replaced the now empty gun, resuming my search for keys. "I think I mean you no harm," I said while I worked, "at least, if you are what I think you are. I hope you mean no ill to me. Just let me go, and say nothing, please."

She spoke again, a short, decisive sentence, and turned and went back to the room. I had no idea what she intended, and so I intensified my search for keys. I had just laid hands on a big ring that had been trapped under the priest's body when he fell, and the nun returned, with a pitcher in her hands. I lifted the keys free, and held them up for her to see.

"I was looking for these, see?" I jangled the key ring in front of her. "That's all I want."

She nodded, which seemed like a good sign. I stood, keeping my hands wide and non-threatening. "If you don't mind, I'll be going now." I gestured back down the corridor toward the library.

The nun nodded again, and said something. She tipped the pitcher, and spilled some water onto the flagstones near the feet of the prone priest. She looked up at me, gestured at the water on the floor, and rattled off a bunch more Greek.

I looked down. If I didn't know better, I would have thought she was trying to help me make the priest think he had slipped and fallen by accident. When he awoke and found the water on the floor, that would be the natural conclusion. I met the eyes of the nun.

"Palm-may," she said. She brushed her hand in the air like she was shooing me away. "Palm-may giddygorah."

"Good enough for me," I said. "Ef charistou." She smiled, and then shooed me away again, more insistently. Needing no more urging, I went.

TWENTY TWO

The problem was, I didn't know exactly where I was going. I continued down the corridor past the library, past the doorway back to the outside, and came to the staircase. I realized that this was the same route we had taken as prisoners earlier that evening. I went down, and emerged into the long hallway that contained the room where I had been held captive not so long ago.

I passed one door on the left and two on the right. I tried the knobs on all three and found that none of them was locked. On the assumption that they would lock the doors of people they wanted to keep captive, I passed quickly on. I was feeling the pressure of not knowing when the fake priest would regain consciousness, nor what he would do when he did. He might find his gun, but sooner or later he was bound to notice his keys were missing, and so I needed to hurry. I passed the corridor that went off to left, the one with the room holding all the girls. They had removed Leyla from that room, as well as me. I would have done the same, in their shoes. From their perspective, it would complicate things if Leyla had a chance to convince some of the girls that they were more or less being sold into the most horrible kind of slavery imaginable, so they would want to keep her separate from them.

I tried the next doorway on the right, and it was locked. I rattled it again.

"Leyla?" I called softly. "Is that you? Leyla?"

I heard a soft moan. I pulled out the key and began frantically trying keys in the lock.

The voice behind the door called out again, this time more clearly. A man's voice.

"Uh-oh," I said.

I stopped messing with the doorknob, and stood still. But the man behind the door called out again. The language was not English, but it was unmistakably a question. I imagined it was saying something like "Who's there, and why are you disturbing me?"

I know it was silly, but for some reason I was inspired to answer in falsetto. "Come out and help me. Please."

The voice spoke again, and I could hear movement in the room, and then the rattle of a key turning in the lock. I waited politely while the door opened, and then hit the man who looked out. This time I caught him more on the temple than the jaw, but the result was the same. When I find a formula that works, I like to stick with it.

I stepped into the room and dragged the recumbent man after me, thankful to see that it was one of the thugs who had searched me earlier that night, and not a genuine priest or nun. He was wearing only boxer shorts. The room was a nun's cell, much like the one where I had been imprisoned. Sitting in the bed was a girl wearing only a bra, with the covers pulled up to her waist. She was staring at me. She looked barely old enough to be in high school. The thug had obviously decided to sample the wares before sending them to market. For a moment, I almost blacked out with rage. I drew back my foot to kick the unconscious man but controlled

146

myself just in time. The girl stared at me in the dim light with wide, frightened eyes.

"Do you speak English?" I asked, breathing heavily, still shaky with anger. I wished now I had hit the thug harder. Much harder.

"A little bit," she said.

"Do you know where they put my wife – the woman who was with me earlier?"

She shook her head, her eyes still wide.

"Get your clothes on," I said. "Come out into the hall, but be quiet."

She nodded, and I left. The thug had made some noise when he fell, slamming the door back on its hinges as he went down. And of course, I had made some sounds of my own, rattling doorknobs and calling Leyla. I hoped no one had heard. As I stepped into the hall, I amended that thought almost immediately. Someone *had* heard, and I was overjoyed that she had.

"Hello?" called a voice in English. "Is anybody there? I heard some noises. What's going on?"

It was the room right next door.

"Leyla," I said at the door. "Not so loud now. Just hang on."

"Jonah?" she called more softly.

"Yes. Hold on a minute."

My hands trembled as I tried the keys. The girl from the other room, dressed now, came out and stood, watching me silently. The fifth key worked. The door opened, and there she was.

After a brief hug, I said, "Hang on."

I went into the room where I had left the thug. Taking the key he had used from inside the room, I locked it from the outside. It might slow him down a little after he woke up.

I turned to the girl. "Do you want to get away?"

She looked at me in puzzlement and shook her head. "I want to go to Italy. I pay to go to Italy. I do not want to stay here."

"In Italy, they will do to you what that man was doing, only many, many times. You will have to do it, even when you do not want to. They will make you a slave."

Her eyes began to tear up. "He said he would make sure I go to the very best place in Italy. He said he would fix everything I need, if I just do this with him."

"He lied."

She shook her head again. "No. I will not be slave. I pay for them to find me a job. I worked very hard to pay them. And now I do this for him. No, they will help me find good place."

"They have a job for you all right." I nodded toward the room. "That will be your job."

"No. You are lying. Why do you say these things?"

"That's a good question," interjected Leyla, laying a gentle hand on the girl's arm. "Ask yourself that. What reason do we have to lie to you about this?"

I took a deep breath. "Look, we have to go. Now. Come quickly."

The girl was crying now, but she shook her head. "No. I go to Italy." She backed away.

"Okay," I said. "Okay. We won't make you. Remember that. We are not making you do anything. But could you do something for us?"

"What is it?"

"We will let you go where you want. But they do not want us to go where *we* want. We just want to go away from here. Please do not tell them about us."

She met my eyes, and then Leyla's. At last she nodded. "Okay."

I took Leyla's arm. "I don't know how much time we've got. Let's get moving."

She didn't argue, but I could tell she wasn't happy about leaving the girl there; neither was I. I turned toward the stairs back up, but just then we heard voices from that direction.

"Other way," I said, and we went back down the hall, past the girl who stood there unmoving like she had nowhere else in the world to go. In a way, I supposed, she hadn't.

TWENTY-THREE

We went past the room where I had been locked up. A few steps farther, the corridor took a right angle turn. The darkness quickly enveloped us.

"Slowly," I said. We don't want to run full speed into a door."

"Or steps," said Leyla, pulling on my arm. "Just here."

I stopped as my left foot came down in space. I pulled back. "Touch the wall on your side, carefully now."

I touched the wall with my left hand, while I held Leyla's hand in my right.

"Feel the wall?" I asked softly.

"Got it."

Slowly we went down. I counted eight steps. At the bottom, I turned and looked back up. The floor of the corridor above was about at the level of my eyes, and it looked lighter than the area where we stood. Suddenly it became very much brighter indeed, when someone turned the electric lights on. We could hear voices approaching down the hall.

Leyla pulled urgently on my hand. In front of us, at the bottom of the steps, was a door. Leyla tried the handle, but it was locked. Pulling my key ring out, I began trying keys, attempting to be both quick and silent. I breathed a prayer of thanks when the second key turned the lock. I kept the key in my fingers as we went through the door, shutting it behind us. Quickly, I locked it again. I hadn't yet removed it from the door when the voices and the footsteps on the other side sounded very close. Both of us stood very still. It sounded like one set of footsteps was coming closer and then running lightly down the stairs. The door in front of us rattled as the man on the other side checked it. He called out to someone further away, and then we heard the sound of receding steps. I put my hand on Leyla's arm, and we continued to stand in silence. I don't know how long we waited, though I'm sure it felt longer than it really was. Just as I was about to move, I heard a cough, just on the other side of the door. The man there called, startlingly loud, and then we heard steps again. This time, I was pretty sure he was really leaving. Leyla squeezed my hand, and we waited some more.

At last I took a step toward her. "Hands on the walls, like before," I breathed softly into her ear. I felt her nod.

We had taken just two strides when we encountered another step. Carefully planting my right foot, I felt for another, but my left foot, ahead of it, came down at the same level. Another two strides, and there was another step. These were obviously wide, shallow stairs, which would have been easier than normal to navigate in the light, but I found them quite frustrating in the dark. We continued following this gently downward-sloping stairway for some time, and it seemed to me that it was also curving slightly to my left.

After a little while, when we should have been be out of earshot, Leyla tugged on my hand. I stopped, and she stepped into the circle of my arms.

"Jonah," she said softly, and I doubt anyone could have heard her ten feet away, "where are we going?"

"I have no idea," I said. "I'm just trying to get away."

"How did you get out in the first place?" she asked.

I hesitated. I knew she'd be mad at me for risking the climb on the cliff, but if I told her now, her response might be softened and distracted by the fact that we still had to make our escape. If I told her later, after we were safe, she might find the leisure to get really angry. So I told her.

"Thank you," was all she said, which threw me off balance almost as much as when I had looked down on the cliff. "What now?"

"I guess we keep going and hope this passage leads us back to someplace where we can sneak out."

"It feels almost like a tunnel to me," she said.

We kept going. The steps quit shortly afterwards, but the floor sloped downward, and the angle began to get steeper. We came to a corner. There were no branching passageways or even doors, just a sharp turn. The darkness was complete, but I imagined a kind of hairpin bend. After that, the tunnel began to switch back on itself frequently, all the while descending steeply. I wondered how far down we had come. Suddenly the smooth wall under my hand turned into rough stone.

"Steps," said Leyla again. "Wait," she added. "There's a handrail on my side."

"Nothing on mine," I said. "Let me go first. That way, if I fall, I won't take you with me."

"What if *I* fall?"

"I'll catch you, and failing that, I'll cushion you."

"Why can't I catch *you*, if you fall?"

"I'm bigger and heavier than you. Also stronger."

"You're just saying that because I'm a girl."

"One of the reasons it's true is because you are a girl."

"Isn't that a little chauvinistic?"

"Do you really want to have this conversation right now?"

"Fine," she sniffed, but kissed my neck as I passed her. "For the record, I'm glad you're bigger and stronger. That means it's your job to kill spiders."

"You think there are spiders in here?"

"Oh, gosh, I wish you hadn't said that. I was thinking of spiders at home. What kind of spiders do they have in Greece?"

"Don't think about it."

The stairs were steep and narrow and continued down for some time. I was very glad of the hand rail, which felt like a piece of iron pipe. I could feel rust in some places. In other places, it felt a little damp. Finally, the railing ended. I stepped cautiously forward and found I was on level, if rough, ground. I could hear a soft sound ahead of me, but I didn't immediately identify it. Another step took me to a door. This one was made of metal. I found the latch, but, predictably it was locked.

"Where do you suppose we are?" asked Leyla. "We must be well below the level of the monastery."

"That's kind of what I'm hoping for," I said. "Maybe this was some sort of escape tunnel built back in troubled times. With any luck, we'll come out somewhere on the hillside, well outside the grounds."

"We have to be beyond the monastery property," said Leyla. "We've come a long way."

I shrugged, which was pointless, because there wasn't enough light to see each other by. But for the first time, I noticed that there was *some* light coming from the cracks around the door.

I fiddled with the keys for a long time, but at last I found the one that worked. The door opened with a loud screech and for a moment, it felt like light was flooding in. I froze, waiting for a shout of discovery. After a few seconds, however, I realized that in fact, the light was quite dim – it was just that we had been in the dark so long. And, apparently, no one had noticed the squealing of the door when it opened.

As we paused, I suddenly identified the soft sound I had been hearing: it was the sound of the sea, washing over rocks. I could make out a short rough passageway, more like a cave than a corridor. Motioning for Leyla to stay put, I crept along until I came to the corner, and cautiously slipped my eye around the edge of the rough wall.

I stood up and called softly to Leyla. She joined me and hand in hand we stepped forward.

We were in a large cavern. In front of us, the moon was reflected off the surface of the water, and we could see the entrance of the cave leading out to the sea beyond. It looked to me like we were facing a little north of due west.

"Jonah, look at where we are standing." Leyla's voice was filled with suppressed excitement.

"Okay."

"Now look here, and over there."

Suddenly, I could see it. "This is the sea-cave we kayaked into a few days ago?"

"The very same. It has to be."

"That's crazy."

"This is the ledge where you sat. You even explored a few feet of the passage we just came out from, but it was too dark to see anything."

"We probably shouldn't hang around too long. Are you up for a moonlight swim?"

"Hold on," she said. She reached up and undid the pins and bands that held her hair up.

"I thought people tended to put their hair *up* before swimming," I remarked.

She ran her fingers through her hair, and then showed me the palm of her hand. She was holding two keys. "The hotel, and the motor-scooter. I hid them in my hair before they searched us."

"Well, aren't you handy to have around?"

"I didn't want them to fall out while I swim. Can you put them in a safe pocket?"

I did. "Maybe we should close and lock that last door again. It might be better if they aren't sure we came this way."

"Let's be quick."

We walked rapidly back through the tunnel to the last door, the one at the foot of the steep, rough stairway. As I began to push it closed, the metal shrieked loudly as it grated on the rough rock of the cave floor.

Leyla put a hand on my arm, and I stopped. "Maybe we should leave it. We don't want anyone to hear."

Even before she had finished speaking, an excited yell sounded from the stairway beyond the door.

"Too late," I said. I heaved, and the door slammed shut with a big, hollow boom. I locked it and grabbed Leyla's hand. Before we reached the water, we could hear more voices, and the door echoed as someone pounded on it.

We stopped at the edge of the water. The mouth of the cave leading out to the ocean was thirty feet away, and I could hear the door behind us scraping on rock as it was pushed open again. Our pursuers obviously had a second set of keys.

"If they have guns, we may not make it out before they could shoot." said Leyla.

"The other cave," I said. "The one you found. Quick!"

I waited until her feet had left the platform, and then dived after her. The water was cold, and it shocked me, but I didn't resurface. Instead, I swam downward, and under the rock wall, resurfacing in the hidden cave that Leyla had discovered a few days before.

"Leyla?" I whispered into the darkness.

"Here."

We fumbled around until our hands met, and then we clambered up onto the rock shelf inside this cave. It was very cold. As I had noticed before, there was a soft breeze coming from somewhere, which made it even colder.

"Look," said Leyla softly.

"I can't see where you are pointing," I said, also keeping my voice very quiet.

She touched my face and turned it. "The water."

Now I could see it. Light was reflecting up through the water.

"They're already at the water's edge in there, probably looking around with flashlights. Do you think they saw us swimming in here?"

"I don't know. Do they even know of this place?"

"I hate it, but all we can do is wait and see," I said.

After a while, the lights went out. I thought it was a good sign that since coming into our refuge, we had never heard them, which meant that the only connection between our cave and the main one was underwater.

"Shall we go?" asked Leyla.

"If I was in their shoes," I said, "I would turn off the flashlight, sit still and wait for a while, just in case the people I was chasing had found some hiding place, and were waiting for me to leave."

Leyla shivered, and grabbed my hand. "I wouldn't have thought of that. The idea of them waiting out there gives me the creeps."

We sat for what seemed like a long time, though probably it wasn't nearly as long as it felt. Just as I was thinking it might be safe to go, we saw the light reflected up through the water again, and Leyla drew in her breath sharply. A few moments later, the light was extinguished again.

"Now what?" asked Leyla.

"Probably, they were doing a final check after their little waiting game. But let's not take any chances. We'll stay a little longer."

I wrapped my arms around her for body heat, and also because I liked her, and we waited again. After what seemed like an eternity, I finally allowed myself to move.

"Let me go out and check," I said. "Count to five hundred. If I'm not back by then, try and see if you can find out where the breeze is coming from, and get out of the cave that way."

We kissed, which was a little awkward in the total darkness, and also hurt my injured lip, which was stinging anyway from the salt water, and then I slipped quietly into the water. I came up in the main cave as quietly as possible, and immediately began to edge to my left, keeping my back to the outer wall of the cave while I looked inward to the rock shelf and the passageway to the stairs and tunnel above. The moon was shining in, but it wasn't at the right angle to reach the back of the cavern. I couldn't hear anything. I took a breath and dove underwater, coming up just short of the rock shelf. There was no one there. I dove back under the wall and resurfaced in our hideaway.

"All clear," I said softly into the darkness.

"Thank goodness," said Leyla. "Let's get out of here."

Back in the main cave, we stayed against the wall until we reached the side of the large opening, and then we slipped quietly out into the moon-washed sea.

TWENTY-FOUR

The water during our daytime swims had been brisk and invigorating. Now it was just plain cold; not Lake Superior-cold, but cooler than comfortable. Because of that, we started out fast, trying to warm up by exercise. After a little while, I veered toward Leyla and touched her. We stopped, treading water.

"We'd better pace ourselves, it's a fair distance around the cliff to the shore."

We set out again in a slow regular rhythm, side by side. Shark attacks are extremely rare in the Mediterranean, but they do happen occasionally, and it seemed to me that if a shark was going to attack someone, night would be a more likely time. I tried not to think about it.

At last, unscathed, but quite tired, my feet touched the rough, large pebbles of the beach. With the moon behind us, we emerged from the water hand in hand, just like in some James Bond movie. For some reason, the reality was not nearly as romantic as the movie scenes I was thinking about.

I stopped at the edge of the beach and brushed at my feet. I untied my shoes from my belt and put them on, even though they were soaking. I left my socks off.

"Jonah, it's only two hundred yards to the hotel."

"I know. But it's cold, and this gravel and rock is killing me."

Leyla was wearing sandals of the type you use when canoeing or river-rafting, so she had never taken them off. Her feet weren't hurting.

We resumed walking toward our hotel. We passed the aquarium, and the large parking lot, and the road up the hill to the monastery. The moon was behind a cloud now, and the landscape around us was dark and mysterious. It was late, and no one was stirring; there were no lights in any of the restaurants or shops. We approached our hotel, and climbed up the stairs. Halfway up, I paused.

"Baby," I said softly, "Do you remember that painting, the cool one on the stair-step shaped board?"

"Yes," she said, matching my quiet tone.

"Where is it?"

She looked around, and so did I. It was no longer on the wall alongside the stairs.

"I don't see it. Does it matter, right now?" asked Leyla.

"I liked it," I said. I couldn't put it into words, but something was bothering me.

I grabbed Leyla's hand and we went slowly back down the steps. We found the painting lying broken into two pieces on the ground near the bottom of the stairs.

"So someone knocked it off the wall by accident," said Leyla.

"Yes. Someone who was in such a hurry that he just let it lie here."

"What does that mean?"

"Let's just look around a minute," I said. Still holding her hand, I led her back to the road, where we could look up toward the

160

balconies of the rooms. I noticed a little red glow up on one of the balconies, but I couldn't be sure which room it was.

"Leyla," I said, "Which room is ours, can you tell?"

She looked up at the dark building looming above us. "I think so. It's the third one from the west, so it would be the one up there with the..." she trailed off and grabbed my arm.

"Jonah, I think someone is up there, smoking on our balcony."

"I thought so too," I said quietly. "That's why I asked. While we were hiding in the cave, someone rushed down here with my room key to wait for us. They were in such a hurry to get here ahead of us that they knocked that painting off the wall."

"What do we do?"

"I thought I'd go help him put out his cigarette," I said. I was feeling a little grim.

"What if there's more than one?"

I was about to tell her that in my present mood, I'd be happy to fight two of them, when something moved on the balcony, and then we could clearly see the shape of a man standing. Unfortunately, it looked like he had seen us at the same time.

He shouted, and to my horror, I heard an answering yell behind us, and the pounding of running feet.

"Quick," I said. "The scooter!"

We raced to where we kept the rented scooter. I pulled the key from my sodden pocket and handed it to Leyla.

"Are you sure?" she asked as she pulled on her helmet.

"Absolutely," I said, buckling mine also. "You're the one for this job."

I had no sooner grabbed her waist, than she threw the bike into gear and we jerked forward with a spray of gravel. Dimly through my helmet, I could hear shouting behind us. And then, to my dismay, I heard an engine, and powerful headlights lit us up.

"They've got a car," I called to Leyla. I have mastered the art of superfluity.

Leyla had opened up the little engine, and we were pulling away. Once the car had a chance to get into higher gears, however, our faster acceleration rate would be meaningless. The tiny engine could never beat any car in flat-out speed.

Leyla wrenched the bike to left, taking a road that appeared to be heading up the steep slopes of Mount Pantokrator. It was good thinking. On a mountainside, and a curvy road, the little bike might still have the advantage. Particularly, I thought, with Leyla driving.

I tried to relax, hold on, and leave her to it. This gave me leisure to curse myself for not thinking ahead. Once the traffickers had failed to find us in a quick search through the convent, the only sensible thing for them to do was get down to our hotel room and wait for us to show up. Since they had my key, finding the hotel and the room number posed no issue whatsoever. It was so blindingly obvious that it had never occurred to me at all.

Leyla was really outdoing herself, and if I wasn't busy with self-recrimination, I might have found the time to be sick. The ride we had taken up the mountain earlier in the week was a slow shuffle in the park compared to the mad, moonlit, headlong rush we were in now. I glanced over my shoulder and found that we had already ascended several hundred feet above our little bay. The headlights of the pursuing car were visible, but they looked quite a ways below and behind. The fact that we had a scooter had taken them by surprise, and the terrain definitely favored our vehicle.

I looked again, and beyond our pursuers was another headlight, possibly a motorbike. I wondered if that was the thug who had waited in our room, joining the pursuit, or if it was some innocent motorist enjoying the soft, late-night air.

After a few more terrifying minutes, we reached the top of the first precipitous ridge, and entered a kind of highland plateau of rolling hills and smaller ridges that stretched up to the summit of Pantokrator. Though the road still curved and changed elevation quite a bit, it wasn't so severe, and I noticed one or two straight stretches of decent length. Once the car behind us made it over the crest, we would begin to lose our advantage.

Leyla braked suddenly, and I slid forward tightly against her. She jerked us quickly to the left and we entered a smaller lane, sheltered by olive trees, with a stone wall on one side. The road curved immediately to the right, and Leyla pulled the bike around the corner, against the wall, and killed the engine. From the main road, under the trees and behind the wall, it would be invisible.

"We can't outrun them on this plateau," she said, whipping off her helmet. "We need to trick them. I almost didn't see this road. Maybe they'll go by."

"It's a big risk," I said.

"I think it was a bigger risk to try to outrun them on flatter ground. Take off your helmet, and put it behind the wall, so it doesn't reflect their headlights."

I did so, and then both of us crouched behind the wall.

It wasn't long before we heard the sound of an approaching engine.

"Rats. I thought we were farther ahead than that," I said.

"That's what I mean," said Leyla. "They would have caught us eventually."

The vehicle came closer, and I could feel myself tensing up. It roared up the little hill just before our turn off, and then around the curve and away, staying on the main road, continuing at full speed.

"Very well done, my love," I said.

"Why, thank you, darling," she said.

We waited a little while longer, and then stood up, buckling on helmets again.

"Now what?" asked Leyla.

"I'm not sure," I said. "Why don't we get on down this road a ways, in case they start to suspect they've been tricked?"

We continued down the smaller road, still quickly, but not at the breakneck speed we had used before. We weren't quite out of sight of the main highway, when I glanced back and saw another light. I began to berate myself with some pseudo-profanity.

"What's wrong?" called Leyla over her shoulder.

"I forgot, there was another motorbike behind them. It might be nothing, but it might be one of them trailing along to catch us doing exactly this."

"Well, let's put some distance between us," said Leyla, and opened up the engine once more. In some ways, this was more terrifying than before. Because we weren't climbing, we were going much faster. In one or two places where the road dipped, I swear we left the ground for a second or two.

As we roared up to the crest of a small hill, I glanced back to see if the other bike was following us on the smaller road. I didn't see him, but I thought I heard a faint tinkling sound that was vaguely familiar. I was still trying to place the noise when we came down the other side of the hill, around a corner.

I don't remember the moment of impact, nor for several moments after. All I know is that I found myself lying on the ground, and the world was fuzzy and out of focus around me. There was a kind of dirty, gray-brown haze in patches of my vision.

I slowly pushed myself up on my elbow, and it was then that I became aware of the blood. The visor of my helmet was splattered with it. It was on my hands, and I could feel the sickly warmth of it on my neck and arms.

I pulled off my helmet. All I could see was blood, and the dirty-gray haze. I didn't feel much pain, and I had a growing, sickening conviction that the blood was not mine. The bike lay on its side about ten feet in front of me and to my right. I looked closer, and saw right next to me the horribly broken body, a mass of torn flesh and blood. So much blood.

TWENTY-FIVE

I began to call Leyla's name, over and over again. I felt for her pulse, but I couldn't even find her wrist. I began to panic. The gray haze seemed to cover her body, and I wondered if it was some sort of weird, psycho-traumatic product of my imagination.

I stood up, looking around wildly for someone, something, anything to help, to make the nightmare end. And there was Leyla, about ten feet to my left, slowly sitting up, groaning and grasping one ankle. I looked down again at the body in front of me.

It was a sheep, or it had been. It wasn't just dead; it was utterly destroyed, and what was left did not smell very pleasant. The gray haze came into focus. It was wool, on the sheep, on the bike, on me, and floating in the suddenly-quiet night air. Another sheep lay still, not too far from Leyla.

I raced quickly to her, helping her remove her helmet.

"Are you okay?" I asked.

"My ankle hurts," she said. "But other than that, I think I'm all right. What about you?" Her eyes grew concerned. "You're bleeding. Badly."

"I don't think so," I said. "I think this is sheep blood, from the first one we hit."

"What about your elbow?"

I looked, and sure enough, I had a scrape on my left elbow. It bled freely, but it didn't look very serious. "It'll keep. Most of this blood belongs to the sheep." I looked around. The other sheep in the herd had not run very far. They were standing in the field about twenty yards away. Some were staring at us, but others were already grazing. I could hear the soft clanking of the bells around their necks as they moved.

"So peaceful," said Leyla. "I think I landed on one when I was thrown clear. At least, most of me did. Somehow, I twisted my ankle."

I looked at her sandal-clad foot. She had her share of scrapes and minor cuts as well. "Can you wiggle your toes?" I asked. She wiggled them.

"What does that mean?" she asked.

I paused. Truthfully, I didn't know. I guess it was just something you were supposed to ask of someone with a leg injury. "I think it means you can wiggle your toes."

She started to chuckle weakly, and then laid back on the ground, laughing some more. "Of all people, I had to marry the guy who makes wise-cracks in moments of crisis."

"Would you rather I panicked?"

"Maybe there is some sort of in-between option."

"Too late," I said. "You already said 'I do.' Besides, this isn't necessarily a crisis."

I helped her sit up again. She grabbed my arm. "Jonah, what's that sound?"

Now I heard it too. It was an approaching motorcycle.

"Okay," I said. "Now it's a crisis."

TWENTY-SIX

I held Leyla under the armpits and half-dragged her to the ditch, with some thought of us lying flat in the field while the rider passed. But just as I got her there, the vehicle came around the same fateful corner. Seeing us, the rider slowed, and then stopped his bike, killing the engine. It was a small motorcycle, nothing fancy, but it would have outrun our scooter. He would have caught us eventually, sheep or no sheep.

I stepped back into the road, putting myself between the cyclist and Leyla, but I didn't say anything. It was just possible that this was an ordinary, legitimate motorist out on an ordinary, legitimate errand in a deserted stretch of countryside at two o' clock in the morning. I like to keep a positive attitude; it makes all the difference.

The man slid off the motorcycle, and his cowboy boots made sharp noises on the smooth surface of the road. I took a step closer to him, trying to keep ready without looking like I was ready. He cocked his head at me, like he couldn't see me properly, which was probably the case, seeing as it was night time and I was covered in blood and patches of fresh wool. He spoke but it was muffled by his helmet. It didn't matter though, because he wasn't speaking English.

"I don't speak...whatever language that is," I said. "Sorry. Ugly American here."

The man rapidly pulled his helmet off. I was close enough to see that he was my height and build, with short, dark hair.

"Borden?" he said. "It is you?"

"Who wants to know?" I asked, but a faint hope was stirring in me.

"Zef. I am Zef."

I could feel a broad grin splitting my face, and I wondered at it. I was being approached late at night on a deserted country road by a known member of the Albanian mob, and for the first time in many hours, I was starting to feel safe.

"Well, now," I said, shaking his offered hand, "that's the best news I've had for some time."

He looked over at Leyla. "Is Mrs. Borden okay?"

Leyla smiled. "Mrs. Borden. I know it'll become ordinary soon, but I still like hearing that."

"Focus, darling," I said. I turned back to Zef. "She hurt her leg. But she can wiggle her toes."

He looked puzzled. "Her toes? She wiggles them?"

"Yes."

"What does this mean?"

"Never mind," I told him.

Leyla could put a little bit of weight on her leg, but not much. She leaned heavily on us as we walked her over to a big rock near the side of the road.

"How did you come to be here?" I asked Zef. "We didn't know ourselves where we were going."

"They let me out of jail yesterday," he said. "I had some things I must do, and I do them. Then, I came to your hotel tonight. You were not there, so I wait – waited," he corrected himself. "While I was there, I see – seed?"

"Saw," I said.

"English is a strange language," he said. "I – saw – some people that I think I might know. Not good people. They would not be guests at your hotel, but one of them, he goes upstairs. The others asked about you. So I wait and watch some more. I think they were waiting for you, so I leave and hide where they do not see me, to see what happens. I saw you come up from the direction of the sea and heard them shout to each other. I saw them get into the car to chase you, so I followed behind on my motorbike."

"How did you know we turned off here?"

"I saw your light, just before you came over the hill. I do not think the others would have saw it."

"Seen," said Leyla. "It *is* a strange language."

"They went ahead a long way before you started again. It was only because I was behind that I seen it."

"Let's leave off the language lessons," I said to Leyla. "I think he was doing better before we started helping him."

"So why did you come to find us in the first place?"

"I wanted to know if you had learned anything more about Lena or Talia. I heard you were released from jail to some American officials, and I wondered if you told them about all of this."

I nodded. "I did tell them. One of them is even part of some sort of international task force on human trafficking."

"Did you tell them about me?"

"A little bit. I told them you were not involved in the human trafficking, but that you might help them. Did they contact you?"

"No."

"I'm not surprised," I said. "They said they had a file on Yakov, and they said he was just a small time brothel owner, who maybe just smuggled in one or two Albanians to work for him. They want to get the 'big fish' as they put it – they want to stop the major gang of human traffickers. But I think they were wrong. In fact, I think Yakov is up to his eyeballs in human trafficking."

Zef put his hand on the back of his head and looked off over the dim landscape. "They were wrong. And they were also right."

"What do you mean?" I asked.

"This last day, I was trying to find out about what you told me when we were in the jail together. There is a man named Yakov, who is said to own that brothel you told me about. But he is not the man you met there, the man with the scar."

"Wait," I said. "The man with the scar is not Yakov? That's the name he gave me."

"Yes. He gave you the name of the brothel owner. He pretended to be Yakov. But that man you met is not Yakov. He is the man in charge of human," Zef paused, searching for the word, "trafficking?" I nodded. "He is the man in charge of human trafficking for the Albanian Mafia."

"But his name is not Yakov?" asked Leyla.

"No," said Zef. "His name is Milot."

"Mee-lote?"

"Yes. Milot." Zef pulled his hand off his head and put it in his pocket. He didn't say anything more.

"So what do we do now?" I asked.

"You should contact those Americans who got you out of jail," said Zef. "Ask them to keep you safe. I will keep looking for Lena."

"But wait," said Leyla. "We found her!"

Zef turned and stared at her like a pointing hound. "You found Lena?"

"Yes. We saw her. We spoke to her."

"You *spoke* to her? What does she say?"

"Maybe we should back up," I said. I told him about our adventures earlier in the night. When I got to the part about all the girls in the big room, Zef interrupted.

"And Lena was there? She was with them?"

"Yes," I said. "She looked a lot like Talia."

Zef nodded. "She does. You said you spoke to her?"

"Zef," I said, "I don't like to say this, but she did not want to escape with us. All the girls are still convinced that they will be taken to a better life in the EU. They don't believe they will be forced into prostitution. I think the traffickers have not done anything to them yet; they are still lying to them. It makes the girls easier to control if they are cooperating willingly until it's too late to go back."

Zef stared sightlessly over the dark plateau. "You told her the truth?"

"We did. She didn't believe us."

"You told her about me, about Talia?"

"Yes."

"I must go and rescue her. Tell me all you can about the convent. How did you escape?"

"Zef," said Leyla, putting her hand on his arm. "I'm so sorry to say this, but I don't think Lena loves you. When we told her that you were looking for her, she didn't seem to care."

Zef nodded, staring off into space again. At last, he shrugged.

"I thought this," he said. "It is not a surprise." He sighed, and then straightened up. "It does not matter. Whatever she thinks, I love her, and I cannot leave her to those –" he said something in Albanian that made me glad I don't understand the language.

"Listen," I said, "we are in a bit of a tough spot here. We were just trying to get away, but the truth is, we don't know where to go. They were waiting at the hotel. If we ask for protection from the police, we might end up with some of those who have been corrupted by Yakov – sorry, Milot. And, anyway, technically, they could lock me up because I didn't stay in Paleokastritsa, like we agreed. Can you help us?"

"I am sorry," said Zef. "I must save Lena. Why don't you get help from the other Americans, the ones who got you out of jail?"

I looked at Leyla. "I don't supposed you memorized the numbers for Jasmine or Joe Williams?"

"No, Jonah, their numbers are on the phone..." she trailed off, comprehension dawning in her eyes. "Oh, no."

I turned to Zef. "The Americans gave me a cell phone with their contact numbers. But I gave the phone to Lena."

Zef's eyes lit up. He was already pulling his own phone out of his pocket. "What is the number?"

"No, you don't understand," I said. "I'm sorry. Of all the useless things I've ever done, this is pretty high on the list. We don't know the number. We didn't write down any of the numbers before we gave her the phone."

Zef slowly replaced his phone.

"Listen," I said. "We might be able to get those numbers. We need to go back to the room and get our computer. We can email our people back in the States, and they can get hold of the people at the embassy, and then they can help us track the phone that Lena has."

"Track the phone?"

"There is a GPS tracker on the phone we gave her. But we need a safe place to do the emailing and to wait for them to contact us."

Zef peered at us in the darkness. "This is all very..." he waved a hand while he looked for the English word, "convenient. You can help save Lena, but you need my help first."

"Oh, sure," I said. "We arranged for you to get the idea to come and see us tonight, and come across the traffickers, and then follow us until we almost killed ourselves hitting a sheep. We're tricky that way." He opened his mouth, but I was getting a little hot under the collar. "Actually, we arranged the whole thing – we made you steal our passports in the first place so that we could trick you into this situation." I waved my hand in disgust. "Just get on your bike and get out of here. We want to have a private lamb dinner and then trick the rest of the Albanian mob into bringing us mint jelly for it."

Zef was already nodding his head. "You are correct, of course. But you must understand. I do not know you. My only concern is to save Lena."

"Who does not love you," said Leyla.

"If I save her only because she loves me in return, is that truly love?" It was hard to see the pupils in his dark eyes. "Is it?"

"No," I said. "You are right. If you truly love her, you will do everything you can for her, even if she does nothing for you." Who knew an Albanian thug would understand real love better than sixty-percent of American church-goers?

"So you understand?"

"I once did everything I could to save someone who said she did not love me," I said, looking meaningfully at Leyla. She nodded slowly. "We both understand."

"You will help me?"

I was still looking at Leyla. She nodded again. I turned to Zef. "We will help you. But we can help you best if you help us get to a safe place where we can communicate with America. This will help us, yes. But it will also help Lena, in the long run."

Zef still hesitated.

"You say you do not know us," I said. "But you and I have fought together. That counts for something." It was one of those weird man-things that I was certain he would understand, though I doubt either he or I could have put it into words. I was almost as certain that Leyla would not understand.

He nodded. "You are correct again. It does mean something." He put out his hand, and I took it. "I am sorry. We will help each other."

TWENTY-SEVEN

The first thing to do was to see if our scooter was still functional. It was covered in blood, and the front fender over the wheel was dented, and pushed back against the tire.

"We got the sheep insurance, right?" I asked Leyla.

When we tried the engine, it started immediately, so we shut it off and went to work on the fender. Zef and I tried to pull it out, but there was no way to get a good grip on the dented area. Then Zef tried to hit the inside of the dent with a rock to knock it back out and free the tire, but there wasn't enough room for both his hand and the rock.

"What about prying it?" I asked. "If we got some sort of stick or something, we might wedge it in and get some leverage."

We stood up, both of us sweating, looking around at the rocky meadow. The nearest tree was half a mile away.

"Why don't you pull it off?"

We both stared at Leyla.

"You know, if you just took that piece off, the tire would be free. It isn't necessary for the operation of the bike, is it?"

"I hate it when she does that," I said to Zef.

He nodded. "You will have a long and happy marriage."

"Do you have any tools?"

He shook his head. "We will have to move it back and forth until it fails."

Working together, we slowly bent and tore the fender away from the bolts that held it over the wheel. It took a lot of sweat and effort, and a few little bits remained, but they would not impede the tire.

Sweating, and shaking a little bit, I walked the bike a few yards down the road. Everything seemed to roll smoothly. The fender had done its job, and saved the tire from bursting, or the wheel from buckling.

"So, to our hotel first, to get our laptop?"

"Yes."

Leyla wanted to keep driving, both so that she didn't become afraid, and also because sitting in front, she had more room to adjust her injured leg. Since it was a scooter rather than a real motorcycle, she didn't need the foot to shift gears or anything. We came down the mountain and stopped under a tree about a hundred yards before our hotel.

"We don't know how long the others will be gone before they come back here," I said to Leyla.

"Yes."

"We don't know if they still have someone waiting in the hotel room."

"No."

"You are injured."

"I understand, Jonah. I'll wait here, on the bike, and at the first sign of trouble, I'll head out of here. You and Zef will meet me at the mountaintop monastery tomorrow at ten AM, if you can."

"But hopefully, we'll just be back here in a few minutes."

"Yes."

We kissed, which still hurt, and then Zef and I slipped into the darkness behind the buildings.

"If you were them, what would you do?" I asked Zef as we watched the balcony, seeing nothing.

"I would have someone there. You might return."

"I think so too. How would you wait?"

"If I was alone, I would wait in the bathroom. When you come in and walk into the main room, I could come out behind you, and keep you from escaping back out the door. If I heard you coming, I might even wait right behind the door."

"And if you had another person to help you?"

"One in the bathroom, and one in the main part of the room, out of sight. After what you have done to Milot's bodyguard, Bekim, and to the two men in the convent tonight, I would certainly have two people waiting for you."

"Only two?" I tried to sound neutral.

Zef shrugged. "They would think to surprise you, or maybe to quickly take your wife hostage to make you behave."

I still had Leyla's room key in my pocket. After more time spent looking at our balcony and sniffing the air for cigarette smoke, we stole up the stairs.

It was impossible to insert the key and turn the lock without making any noise at all. Once it was unlocked, I nodded at Zef. He opened the door and walked in, past the bathroom and into the main room, making plenty of noise. I stepped inside the room noiselessly and allowed the door to close, waiting just inside the room, the bathroom doorway ahead of me, to my left.

After about four painfully loud heartbeats, a figure emerged from the bathroom. I jumped him from behind, and immediately wrapped my left arm around the front of his neck, holding my wrist in the crook of my right elbow, with my right hand behind his neck to lock it in. The man struggled wildly and bent forward to try and throw me off. I kicked his feet from under him, and we fell to the ground with him on top, but my choke-hold intact. The main pressure was on the sides of his neck, compressing his carotid arteries and shutting off blood flow to the brain. After several more seconds he went limp and I released him. He would be out for a while, and would wake up with a massive headache, but otherwise he would be fine.

I got up as Zef stood, watching me without comment.

I looked beyond him into the main room. "Only one?" I asked.

"Do not be insulted," he said. "Remember, most people do not expect a good fighter to look..." he seemed to be searching for the right words, "like you."

"Thanks, I wasn't insulted," I said. "At least, not until you said that."

Our room was a disaster. The mattress was halfway off the box-spring, and our clothes were scattered everywhere. I wasn't sure what they had been looking for, but after looking a little bit myself, I realized our laptop computer was gone, as well as both of our tablet readers.

"They probably want to make sure that you did not leave behind any record of what you have been experiencing. It also prevents you from emailing anyone."

"Yeah, but it's still rotten. I had five hundred books on my tablet."

Our luggage had been searched, but was undamaged. We had a small backpack, and Leyla had a big over-the-shoulder bag. I stuffed a bunch of clothes, toiletries and some odds and ends into them, and then turned to Zef.

"Let's go. Leyla's waiting."

We returned to where we had left the bikes. I was kind of holding my breath, but Leyla was there, unharmed and alone. I handed her a container of ibuprofen and a water bottle.

"Thank you," she said. "It's really starting to hurt."

"They took our computer and the tablets."

"That's going to make it hard to contact Alex. Do you remember his email address?"

"Not off the top of my head. But we can deal with that later. Right now, we need to get you to a safe place."

Leyla was looking through the bags I had brought.

"Did you get the hair dryer?" she asked.

I stared at her.

"There would have been room in here."

"I did not get the hair dryer," I said. "I did manage to subdue the thug who was waiting for us, however."

She nodded. "I'll make do. Just try to remember it next time."

I stared at her again, while she returned my look calmly. Just before I looked away, she winked.

"You are a piece of work," I said.

"I know," she said. "Isn't that why you married me?"

"No, it was for your dimples."

"Oh, right, I forgot."

I turned to Zef, who had a slightly bemused look on his face. "What's the plan?"

Zef seemed apologetic. "I do not know many good people," he said. "I am in the Mafia. But Talia's mother, Marsela, is the sister of my own mother. She and my uncle Skender are good people. I can take you to them."

"But Yakov – sorry, Milot, knows where they live," I said. "That's where they picked me up before. They were watching their house."

Zef nodded. "Yes, I know. This is what I have been doing since I was released from the jail. I found them and brought them to a safe place, where Milot will not find them."

"Okay," I said. "We don't really have many options, anyway."

Leyla continued to drive the scooter, because it was easier on her leg. Following Zef, we ascended the ridge just to the north of Paleokastritsa for the second time that night, though on a different road. We spent a brief few kilometers on the crest. Below me in the moonlight, I caught sight of another bay, much wider than the one we had come from, with a long curved beach facing the ocean to the west. Nestled on the shore was a small town. Shortly, we began to descend again. It took some time, I felt a little cycle-sick from the switchback road, but eventually we were in the outskirts of the town. I saw a sign, and my Greek was good enough to translate it from Greek letters into *Agios Georgios*, or, "Saint George." The town had less of a touristy feel than Paleokastritsa, and there wasn't much traffic at this time of night, but there were a number of cars parked along the sides of the road, presumably near rental houses. Zef pulled into a small lane lined with cypress and olive trees, and shortly after that into a small parking area in front of a stucco house with a tile roof. Following his example, we killed our engine and pulled off our helmets.

"There are many tourists here this time of year, but it is more remote than many other places in Corfu. I do not think Milot will look here, and even if he did, he could not simply ask about strangers – there are too many visitors."

"Good thinking."

Zef knocked firmly, and after a long while, the door opened to show Skender, sleep tousled, at the door.

After a quick exchange in Albanian with Zef, he stood aside. "Please come in," he said to us.

The house was small, but neat, with tile floors and thick, plastered walls. It held two bedrooms.

"We thought maybe Talia would be joining us soon," said Skender, sadly, as he showed us into the second bedroom. I helped Leyla into the room, sitting her down on the bed.

"I guess you'll have to call the States," I said. "That's probably better, anyway; it will be faster."

"If we can find a phone." She met my eyes. "You have to go with him, don't you?"

I held her gaze for a long time. "*That* is one real reason I married you," I said at last. "You don't like it, but you understand, at least a little."

"You are who you are. That's why *I* married *you*. I can't help worrying, but I don't want you to change."

I put my arms around her, and she slipped hers around me. We stayed that way for a long time.

"Come back to me."

"Always."

TWENTY-EIGHT

Zef and I were back in Paleokastritsa. We were situated on the north side of the big parking lot near the aquarium. The little half-moon bay with the main swimming beach, and the road up to the monastery, were in front of us. To our right was the bay that Leyla and I had emerged from earlier in the night. To our left was our hotel. The moon hung low over the water, but we could still see the land and sea pretty well.

We had been there for some time, watching and waiting. We had agreed to scope things out for a while and consider our options before doing anything rash. I was finding it almost as boring as being locked in a room in a convent. Zef stirred at last.

"They will have to move the girls sometime," he said. "That will be the best time to act. You are certain there is no other way out?"

"I know you haven't been here before, but take a look." I gestured. "The convent is on a peninsula. Except for the little piece of land we're looking at, it is completely surrounded by water. Also, except for the hillside which we can see in front of us, it is all cliffs. That means, except for the way Leyla and I escaped, we are looking at the only way in or out..." I trailed off, realizing what I had said.

"The sea-cave," said Zef.

"I'm sorry," I said. "I am very tired, but it was a stupid mistake."

"Can you see the entrance to the cave from here?"

"No, it is too far around."

"Is there any location where we can watch the road here, and also the sea cave?"

I looked around. Finally, I pointed to the top of the cliffs that formed the northern barrier of the bay to our right. "Up there."

Zef shook his head. "We could not get back down quickly enough to do anything."

"The only other place is about the middle of that bay." I gestured to our right. "If we could walk on water, we could wait there."

"A boat?" His tone was mild.

"Of course. I tell you, I'm tired. We could run it in to shore here if they come down the road. If they come in their own boat, we can follow."

"Do you know how to drive the boat?"

I had grown up near Puget Sound, and spent many happy weekends on the water. Now, living on Lake Superior, I still spent a certain amount of time in motor vessels. "Sure," I said. "I can drive the – I mean, I can pilot a boat, yes."

Zef stared at the rocky peninsula in front of us. He seemed to come to a decision. He pulled out his phone, dialed, and spoke in Albanian for a moment. There seemed to be some back-and-forth exchange in the conversation, and then he seemed excited. He said, "Falamendjerit," and hung up. He dialed again, and waited a long time, and finally began speaking again. He seemed to be asking a number of questions. This time, at the end he said "Ef charistou." I now knew that he was thankful to an Albanian person and also a Greek person. Jonah Borden, ace detective.

"Come quickly," he said.

We mounted his motorcycle, and I had to hold on as he quickly accelerated away from our spot, away from the hotel, back towards Corfu Town. We didn't go far, however. We took a right hand turn and raced down toward the main harbor of Paleokastritsa, where hundreds of boats bobbed in the sheltered marina. Zef slowed, and appeared to be counting as we moved along the frontage road.

"Hold on," he said, and turned the bike onto one of the long docks. About two-thirds of the way down, he stopped. We got off, and he led the way to a berth holding what I would call a walk-around — a big motor boat with the wheel up on a tiny bridge and protected on all sides but the back. There was some open space in the cockpit behind the wheel, and a small cabin forward and below the wheel. The deck up front was covered and formed the roof of the cabin. It was a dual purpose vessel, used for fishing and also for cruising on short one or two night trips. Zef jumped on board and rummaged around until he came up with a key.

"Can you drive it?"

"Sure," I said. "Get those ropes off."

As Zef went to cast off, I took the key up to the bridge and sat in the captain's chair. The engine started right up. The rumble sounded satisfactorily powerful. I flicked on the navigation lights and slowly guided us out of the marina, while Zef climbed up in the seat next to mine. Once we were past the last navigation buoys, I pushed the throttle forward all the way. We leaped toward the northwest, our wake forming three clean, wide, white stripes in the dark water.

It didn't take us long to get back to the northernmost bay of Paleokastritsa. I cut the throttle back and brought us around until we could see both the road down from the convent, and the cliff face that held the cave from which Leyla and I had escaped.

"We'll have to anchor," I said. "We could burn a lot of fuel holding position here, and it would probably draw unwanted attention if we leave the engine running."

Thankfully, the boat was set up with an electric winch, which would make getting the hook back up relatively quick. I made some quick estimations of wind and tide, and dropped the anchor. Before long we were swinging in place, still in view of everything we wanted to see.

"You sleep," said Zef. "I will call you."

"You need sleep, too," I said.

"If we travel by water, you will have to drive the boat," said Zef. "I can sleep then."

"And if it is by land?"

He shrugged. "It does not matter. I would not sleep now, anyway."

I was too tired to argue any more. There was a very small but neat cabin in the bow, with two padded seats that doubled as bunks. I stretched out and was asleep before I could kick my shoes off.

TWENTY-NINE

I felt a hand on my shoulder, and opened my eyes. I had no idea where I was.

"Borden."

It was Zef.

The cabin seemed bright with light coming from overhead. I glanced up to see a skylight showing me a deep blue atmosphere.

"It's already light. What time is it?"

"About ten in the morning."

"What happened? Did you fall asleep?"

"Nothing has happened yet. Except, perhaps something happens now. Come."

I followed him out to the open back of the boat. We were stern-on to the peninsula that held the convent. The sun was already high, and there were a number of boats out on the water. Some were anchored near us, while others were cruising farther out to sea. Zef pointed toward the cliffs.

"There."

It was a long, open-decked pontoon boat lined with benches, shaded with a canopy. The benches were empty, but looked like they might seat twenty people. At thirty Euros a head for a cave tour, it would be a money-making machine for its owners.

"I found these in the boat," said Zef, and handed me a pair of binoculars.

Looking through them, I could see the pontoon boat in more detail. The engine on the back was a fifty-horse Johnson outboard, about right for moving a bunch of passengers up and down the coast and around the pretty little coves of Corfu, though it certainly wouldn't win any races. "It's just a cave-tour boat. There are several groups doing those tours. I think someone tried to get Leyla and me to ride that boat our first day here."

"Look again," said Zef.

I was still fuzzy with sleep, and, I realized, craving coffee. "Just tell me," I said.

"Why is it empty?"

It was true. The only person on the vessel was the man at the wheel. I tried to get my head around it. Why would the owners send it out to the caves with no one in it?

"Is there any coffee on this tub?" I asked.

"I do not think so," said Zef. "However, there is Coca-Cola in the refrigerator."

"I'll be back," I said. I ducked back into the cabin, opened the tiny fridge and took a Coke for me, and one for Zef. I handed it to him as I came back on deck.

"Is that the cave where you were with Mrs. Borden?" He pointed.

"I think so," I said. The pontoon boat was moving slowly in that direction. "So why do you think the boat is empty?"

"I do not know. But it is unusual, and it is happening near the convent. I do not think it is by mistake."

"It would be a big coincidence, I agree."

We watched the boat as it slowly maneuvered toward the cave.

"Let's think this thing through," I said. "So, they bring the girls to Corfu, because it is close to the Middle East, Eastern Europe, and the EU."

"Shouldn't you prepare to follow that boat? Raise the anchor?"

"No, we can outrun that boat no problem. They won't get away from us if we need to follow." I took another swig of Coke. It was black, and it had caffeine, I'll say that for it. "So, thinking out loud again. They bring the girls to Corfu, as you told us, because it's conveniently close to the homelands of the girls, and to the EU?"

"Of course," said Zef. "But why bring them to the convent here?"

"Well, you expect to see a large number of women together at a convent. And people don't usually look closely at nuns – it is rude to stare, and often nuns make people uncomfortable anyway. So, a lot of nuns traveling to a convent, and staying in a convent, does not draw too much attention. My question is, why *this* convent? You'd think there would be other convents on Corfu."

"I do not know," said Zef. "I am not a religious person."

"How would you get the girls to the EU from here, if you were doing it?"

"It is only about one-hundred and twenty kilometers across the sea from here."

"Seventy miles. That makes sense. Airports have security and require passports and visas."

The pontoon boat slowly disappeared into the cave's mouth.

"There," said Zef. "They come from the convent into the cave where you escaped, get into that boat, and they are taken to Italy from there."

"No way," I said. "You'd have to be crazy to try the open sea with that boat. Loaded with people, they couldn't hydroplane, and with any kind of wave action, the deck would be underwater in a heartbeat. If it is really well made, the weight of all that water on deck might not tear it to pieces, but I wouldn't bet on it. If the deck survived that sort of beating, when all the water comes over the front, the stern will go up and pull the propeller out of the water, and they would lose power. With any sort of bad weather at all, out in the middle, they'd be underwater in minutes."

"So what is happening here?" asked Zef, gesturing at the cave.

"That's what we're here to find out," I said. "I guess we'll get the hook up." I started the engine and we raised the anchor. About the time we were done, the pontoon boat re-emerged from the cave.

"See!" said Zef, pointing.

The boat was fully loaded with what looked like tourists. They had on floppy hats and loud shirts; cameras hung around their necks. It looked like any one of a half dozen vessels taking tourists up and down the coast into caves. Except, of course, that in this case, it was taking tourists *out* of a cave, and every one of them was female.

"So they bring them in as nuns, to disguise the fact that they are being smuggled," I said. "And then they dress them as tourists and take them out again. Why not dress them as tourists in the first place? And why not just take them back down the hill – why the trip in the boat?"

"Obviously, I do not know," said Zef.

"I wasn't really asking you," I said. "Just thinking out loud."

"I am also thinking out loud," said Zef. "And I am thinking I do not understand why they do this."

"Okay. They want them on the water, but they do not want them to be really noticed on the water. They aren't going to Italy, not in that thing, so where *are* they going?"

The pontoon boat was out of the cave now, and moving past us toward the north, crossing the bay to seaward of us. I noticed the fishing rods that were stowed on our boat.

"Let's go fishing," I said.

"Why would we do this?" asked Zef.

"We don't know where they are going, so we need to follow them. However, our boat would normally go much faster than they can go. If we go along slowly behind them, they will wonder why, and become suspicious. But, if we were fishing, that would give them a reason for why we are going so slowly."

"So we fish so that they do not become suspicious?"

"Exactly."

"I do not know how to go fishing," said Zef with a frown.

"Dang. I was almost starting to like you," I said. I nosed us out to sea until we were well out of the bay, and then put the boat in neutral. We could see the pontoon boat, still pushing northward. I took one of the poles down from its rack. A large Rapala-type lure was already rigged on it, and some gear to keep it swimming quite deep. I dropped the lure into the water, and showed Zef how to work the big bait-casting reel.

"Let out the line until I tell you," I said. He seemed to understand what I had showed him. I moved us forward slowly, and he clicked the reel over when I told him. Now I had an excuse to go slow as we followed the pontoon.

To our right, the coast of Corfu reared up into the steep cliffs that marked the end of the big ridge that separated Saint George from Paleokastritsa. The pontoon was getting farther ahead of us, but I wasn't concerned; it was still easily visible.

Zef gave a sudden shout, and I looked back to see him holding the rod with both hands as it bent over. I pulled the boat back into neutral, and climbed down to the deck beside him.

"Pull the rod straight up," I told him, "and then put it down, reeling as fast as you can. Then pull it up again and repeat."

I could hear the drag on the reel clicking as he pulled, meaning he had on a pretty decent-sized fish. I hunted around and found a fighting belt that allowed a fisherman to seat the rod in a leather cup in front of the waist. The alternative was to brace the rod on a hip or thigh, and with a big fish, this could mean bruising. I strapped the belt around him, giving him tips as he fought the fish. It took about fifteen minutes for him to bring it in – it was a large tuna. I let Zef look at it, and then set it free without taking it out of the water.

"That was extremely enjoyable," said Zef, his face red and his breath coming a little fast. "Do you suppose there are more down there?"

More than one person has suggested to me that fishing will be my downfall, and it hit me suddenly that perhaps it was. "The pontoon!" I yelled, and leaped back up to the wheel, shoving the throttle forward.

After Zef had put the rod down and unstrapped the fighting belt, he climbed up next to me.

"I do not understand how I could forget about Lena and what we are doing here," he said.

"I do. Don't take it too hard. I have the same problem."

He glanced once over his shoulder, with a slightly longing look, and then began scanning the area in front of us with the binoculars. I couldn't see the pontoon boat anywhere. After a moment, he put the glasses down.

"I do not see them"

"They must have rounded a point or something. There," I gestured. Several miles away the coast line began to bend away to the right into the big bay that held Agios Georgios.

"Wait!" cried Zef, pointing himself.

Just ahead, the cliffs opened up to the sea, forming a tiny cove. There was no way to reach it by land without climbing down the rocky crags.

In the little bay was a large, double-hulled power catamaran; maybe fifty feet long by twenty or twenty-five wide. The pontoon boat appeared to be moored to the stern of the big yacht. Zef brought the field glasses to his face.

"They are getting the girls off the small boat and putting them on the big one," he said. He brought the binoculars down and looked at me. "Can the big boat go to Italy?" he asked.

It was all making sense now. "Absolutely. Put that rod back up in the holder," I told him, slowing down. "From a distance, it will look like we are trolling." I slowed down, and then picked up the binoculars myself. The big cruising catamaran had a swimming deck off the stern. The girls were being helped from the pontoon onto this, and then up into the yacht. At a rough guess, I figured the catamaran could hold fifty-or sixty people. It wouldn't necessarily be comfortable, but it probably could handle that many safely. I scanned the vessel a bit more. It was built for pleasure cruising, much like a dozen or more big yachts I had seen in the area. It was the type of vessel owned by wealthy people, or by tourist companies. There was nothing about this vessel that would draw attention to itself as unusual.

I trolled on past the bay.

"What shall we do?" asked Zef, once the other boats were hidden again by the cliffs on either side of the cove.

"Did you see Lena when you were looking at them?"

"I did not."

"Then we don't know if she is on board that yacht yet. We can't do anything until we know where she is. I think there were almost four dozen girls in the convent last night. That will mean at least three more trips with that pontoon boat to get them all on the yacht. We've got time."

Zef had the number of Marsela's cell phone. We called it and then spoke to Leyla to fill her in. She hadn't been able to reach Alex, or anyone else, yet.

"What are you going to do?" she asked.

"We don't know yet."

"Be careful, Jonah."

"Always. I love you."

"And I love you," she said.

We hung up.

"We are going to watch them?" asked Zef.

"Do you have a better plan?"

"Of course not," he said. "However, perhaps it would be better if we do not appear suspicious. It seems best that we fish again."

I looked at him. He appeared to be just a little casual. I began to grin. "We'd be fools not to," I said.

THIRTY

It took three trips, as I had thought, which made me feel slightly smug about my ability to predict the logistics involved in major criminal enterprises. There was always an alternative career path for me in crime, if the God thing didn't work out. It took about three hours total, which we spent fishing. After the third pontoon had left, we saw through the binoculars that the catamaran was raising anchor.

"Now what?" asked Zef. He had caught another, smaller tuna, and a pretty decent barracuda. I myself had picked off two barracuda. He looked kind of regretful as we stowed the fishing gear. "That was very enjoyable."

"Well, we could keep fishing. Or, if you felt like it, we could maybe rescue fifty girls who are about to be sold into a life of sex-slavery, including the woman you love."

"I do not think you are as funny as you think you are."

"A lot of people have mentioned that to me over the years."

"Do we go get Lena now?"

The catamaran was already moving. "I don't think we can," I said. "We have no way to make them stop. We can outrun them, but it does us no good – we can't get on their boat. We're going to have to see where they're headed."

I pushed the throttle forward. There was a GPS navigation unit next to the wheel. I couldn't read the Greek menu, but everything else looked pretty normal. I zoomed out until I could see Italy.

"Let's get ahead of them a little bit, so they aren't suspicious," I said. "They might notice if we followed them, but if they are the ones following us, I doubt they'll suspect."

"How do you know where to go?"

"I don't, but let's take a look."

Looking at the GPS, the closest place in Italy was the very tip of the "spiked heel" of that country. There was a town there called Leuca. I peered at the unit, and zoomed in a little.

"Keep an eye on that catamaran."

I pushed the throttle forward, but not all the way. I was certain we could go faster than the fully loaded yacht, and I wanted to make sure they were headed our direction.

As we moved farther out from the coast of Corfu, it became obvious that the catamaran was indeed headed in the same general direction. Zef and I kept looking back through the binoculars. Because the cat was a wide boat, it was easier to tell, even at a distance, which way it was pointed. I made numerous small adjustments, staying ahead of them, but moving more or less on the same course.

After a while, we settled into a pretty comfortable rhythm, occasionally making little course corrections, but mostly plowing through the ocean at about eighteen knots, holding position roughly a mile ahead of the big catamaran. Corfu slowly sank into the sea behind us. Italy was not yet visible ahead, but the GPS assured us it was there. At this speed, it would take us about four hours to get there.

Zef leaned back and put his cowboy boots up against the side of the boat. "So," I said, leaning back myself, and wishing we had some food along, "What's with the cowboy boots?"

"I do not understand."

"Why do you wear cowboy boots?"

"I like them."

"That's it?"

He was quiet for a moment. "My father deeply enjoyed American cowboy movies. When I was very young, he used to take me to the theatre and see them."

"The communist government allowed cowboy movies?"

"I was only five years old when the communist rule was ended. Even before it was over, things were changing."

"So you liked the movies?"

"Yes. My father said the cowboys were strong, admirable men, and I thought so too. Then, not long after Albania stopped being a communist country, he found a pair of small cowboy boots in the market, and bought them for me."

"That's cool. Your father sounds like a good dad."

"He died not long after."

I looked at Zef. There did not seem to be much emotion, but he was in a much more talkative mood than I had yet seen.

"I'm so sorry. Is that why you ended up joining the Albanian mob?"

"Mob?" asked Zef.

"Mafia. It is American slang for any organized crime group."

"Of course," said Zef. He stared out over the ocean in front of us. "My father died when I was eight years old. My mother tried very hard, but as I grew, I became – difficult. I kept fighting at school and with the other children in our apartment building. One day, I got into trouble again at school. I was sent to the office. Usually, it was my mother who came to the school on such occasions, but this time, when I was about twelve years old, it was my uncle." He raised the binoculars and turned, checking to make sure the catamaran was still on the same course.

"I did not know my uncle very well. Even though he was the brother of my father, my father did not let us spend time with him, and mother also kept me away after father died. But when he came to the school that day, my uncle was very kind to me. I admired him greatly. After that, he began to spend time with me. He told me that my mother did not understand what it was to be a man. He did not stop me from fighting; instead, he showed me how to do it better. We did not tell my mother about it – she thought I was in a club after school, but really, I was with my uncle all the time. Soon, the other children who fought with me began leaving me alone."

My stomach was rumbling. "Hold that thought," I said. I switched on the autopilot and went below. There was still plenty of Coke in the fridge. I also found some cheese. In the cupboards I found a can of chick-peas. I brought two Cokes, the cheese, a knife, and a can-opener to the bridge, handing one of the drinks to Zef.

"Go on," I said, opening a Coke.

Zef also popped the tab on his drink. "When I was fifteen, my mother died, and I went to live with my uncle. I began to see that he had many men who worked for him, and they were all afraid of him. This made me admire him even more. At first, he did not tell me about his business. I only knew that many men worked for him and that they were afraid."

I sliced some cheese and handed it to him, and he went on. "One day, not long after I was done with school, my uncle asked me what I planned to do for work. I told him I did not know. He asked me to come along with him in his business the next day." Zef bit into the cheese, stared at it, looked at me, and then spit over the side of the boat. "That is terrible."

I nibbled a corner of the cheese and formed much the same opinion. I wasn't *that* hungry. I threw the rest over the side.

We washed our palates with some Coke. I waved my hand. "You went with your uncle to his work one day."

"Yes. He told me a man had borrowed money from him and did not want to give it back. I was naturally very angry about this – it is not right. We went to see the man. When we got there, he did not have the money. My uncle threatened his family, and the man grabbed a knife and rushed toward my uncle. I stopped him and beat the man for trying to hurt my uncle. After that, my uncle got me a job working for the betting parlors, collecting debts."

"And you've been doing that ever since?"

"Yes. Over time, I found out about some of the other things my uncle does – his other businesses – and I did not want to get involved in them. The betting parlors are the best place for me. No one makes those people come in there and lose their money. If they choose to do it, they should pay."

"Your uncle sounds like an interesting man."

Zef nodded. "He is interesting. But he is not a good man."

"It sounds like he was good to you."

"In a way, perhaps. He gave me a place and he showed me some things about how to be a man. But he is a hard man. He does not tolerate weakness – he crushes it when he sees it. He does not know about compassion. I do not think he knows anything about love."

There it was again. This hard, young mobster talking about love. I looked at him more closely, but his face was expressionless, as it was most of the time.

"Why do you think he took you in, gave you a place?"

"I do not think it was love. I believe he gave me a place because he thought to make use of me. Perhaps, in some small way, he also wanted to have pride in his family. It wasn't love. It was a chance to show his rivals that he was creating a strong family. He does not have any sons."

I was quiet. Throughout my life, I had rarely regretted not speaking. After a moment, Zef spoke again.

"Because of this, my uncle was very disappointed when I wanted to stay in the betting parlors. But I did not want to be involved with drugs and... and prostitution."

There was a little catch to his voice. His face was still impassive. "Zef," I asked quietly, "what is your uncle's name?"

There was a long silence. Finally, he turned to me. "Milot. My uncle is Milot."

THIRTY-ONE

For a long time, there didn't seem to be much to say. I checked to see that the catamaran was still behind us. Finally, I said, "Does your uncle Milot know about you and Lena?"

Zef was staring at the empty horizon where Italy would eventually appear. He nodded.

"Did he entice her into leaving Albania?"

"What is 'entice'?"

"Trick. Was he the one who made this happen?"

Zef nodded again. We were quiet for a while.

"He thought perhaps that Lena was making me soft. He thought she was the reason I would not work in the other areas of his business." He finished his Coke with a long swig and crumpled the can slowly, unconsciously. "First, he sent someone to tell her bad things about me. I was able to convince her they were lying – at least at first. Then, Milot sent a very handsome, charming man to spend a lot of money on Lena. He took her to nice places and treated her very well. One night, he got her drunk and slept with her. Milot showed me pictures. At first, I was very angry, and broke up with her, but then, a friend who also works for Milot told me what Milot had done. I tried to make things better with Lena, but then Milot did this."

"Did you know he was into human trafficking?"

"No. I did not realize he was behind all this until you told me."

"*I* told you?"

"It was in the jail, when you told me about the man you had met in the brothel. You said his name was Yakov, but you described Milot. He has a scar on his face like you said."

I finished my own Coke. "Does he know you are in the middle of all this?" I asked, waving my hand. "I never mentioned your name to him."

"I do not think he knows yet," said Zef.

We traveled without speaking for a long time, lulled by the dull roar of the engine and sound of the waves. I started day-dreaming about a big, juicy cheeseburger. At last, Zef said, "In a way, perhaps Milot is right. I have learned things from Lena, from Talia, and from Marsela and Skender that I never learned from Milot. Perhaps they *were* the reason I stayed in the betting parlors."

"Do you think what you learned from them was good?"

"Yes. Milot does not know everything."

I nodded. "I'll agree to that. For one, love is not weakness."

Zef was quiet.

After another hour or so, we saw a dark smudge ahead. Gradually it coalesced into land, and after we had been going for about three hours total, we could see brown hills ahead, well above the horizon now.

"How do you know where on the coast they are going?" asked Zef.

"I don't. That's why we need to do a little more fishing."

I pushed the throttle forward, and as Italy grew closer and closer, we pulled so far ahead that the big yacht behind us was barely visible over the horizon. Abruptly, I cut the engine back to neutral.

"Poles," I said.

Zef did not need encouragement. Very quickly, we had two poles out, and I began trolling in a very long oval that took us across the path of the oncoming boat.

"Soon they will pass us, believing we are simply fishing again. Once they are a little ways ahead, we'll follow them in to the coast."

I tried to judge it well, and felt a glow of satisfaction as the boat passed us almost a mile to the east, while we were trolling toward the west. I swung around wide to the north and back east again, keeping them in sight, but allowing us to fall behind while we stayed at trolling speed. When they were a good mile to the north of us, we began to reel in the lures.

"Fish!" yelled Zef suddenly.

I looked ahead. The catamaran was rapidly getting smaller as it pulled away. "Cut it," I said.

"Cut the line?" asked Zef. He seemed confused.

"Cut it. We don't have time."

"But..."

"Cut it."

Reluctantly, he pulled out a knife and severed the line. I swung the boat in behind the catamaran and began to follow it. I made up a little distance, just to be sure we didn't lose them, but stayed about a mile behind.

"That was very disappointing," said Zef, climbing up beside me.

I smiled, and said nothing.

"I think it was a very big one."

I turned to look at him. "Congratulations."

"Why do you say this?"

"You've become a true fisherman."

THIRTY-TWO

The coast of Italy approached rapidly now, and soon we began to distinguish cliffs rising from the sea. The boat ahead of us headed straight towards the wall of broken rock. I slowed as we approached the shore, dropping further back, waiting to see which way the catamaran would turn.

The catamaran didn't turn. It kept roughly straight on. I raised the binoculars to my eyes. I looked carefully to make sure. "You've got to be kidding," I said.

"I did not say anything," said Zef.

"It's an expression. It means: 'this is unbelievable.'" I handed him the binoculars. "Scan the base of the cliffs."

"Caves," he said slowly. "Just like in Corfu."

"Exactly."

"Do you suppose they have a tunnel to one of those caves from someplace at the top?"

"I'll bet you dollars to donuts they do."

"I do not bet; I only collect from those who do."

"Whatever. See if you can find a cave with a house or some sort of building at the top of the cliff above it, or close by." I cut the throttle way back, so we were barely making way through the crisp blue water. "Start by looking in the direction they're headed."

"There," said Zef, pointing. He handed me the glasses.

Unlike the cave below the convent at Corfu, this one had a clear approach, with deep water all the way up to the cliff face. The opening was larger, too, though not quite high enough to accommodate the yacht that carried the girls. I swung the binoculars up, traversing a cliff that was maybe a hundred feet high. The buildings were not right on the cliff edge, but were set back on the slope above, maybe one hundred yards or so from the precipice. I couldn't tell, but it looked like at least two structures: a large dwelling, and maybe a big garage or storage building. Olive, cypress, and palm trees obscured my view. I looked back at the yacht. They were close in to the cliffs now and definitely maneuvering toward that particular cave.

I marked the spot on the GPS and turned us to the southwest, toward a town that the unit told me was called Leuca.

"What are you doing? They are right there."

"We can't hang around anymore without arousing suspicion. I've marked the spot on the GPS, so we can find it again with no problem. For now, we've got to pretend we're moving on, or they might not unload the girls."

"Do we want them to unload the girls?"

"Well, we can't rescue them while they're on that boat. We covered that before: we have no way to make it stop. I'm thinking we wait a while, give them time to unload, and then call the Italian police."

Zef was shaking his head. "It is no good. Milot will be paying some of the police here, just as in Corfu, and in the same way, we cannot know who it might be. If we call them, we might get one who works for him, and end up dead."

"So we're on our own."

Zef looked at me, his brown eyes calm and serious. "You do not have to help me. You have done much already, more than I have done for you."

I rubbed my chin, looking at him. Finally, I shook my head. "I'd have a hard time looking in the mirror if I just abandoned you, Lena, and Talia at this point. I think I'd better see this through."

Zef nodded with his normal lack of expression. "I thank you."

"So for now," I said, "we head toward Leuca to keep them from suspecting our boat. We'll come back in a couple hours, go into that cave, and see where it takes us."

THIRTY-THREE

It still was not fully dark when we returned, staying in as close to the cliffs as I dared, so that we would not be detected from above. The sky still glowed with the memory of the sun's presence, and the clear water was a deep, mysterious purple in the deepening dusk.

I should have been nervous, but I was far too hungry for that. I found myself thinking that if we hurried up and rescued Lena, we could motor down to Leuca and get something to eat before the restaurants closed.

I figured the big catamaran would not hang around. If I were running the human trafficking operation, I would want as few people as possible to see my transport boat near the drop-off point. Most people going by while the boat unloaded would assume they were seeing a party-boat checking out the cave, but if it stayed too long, it would draw unwanted attention.

We stopped before we reached the deep cove that held the cave where the catamaran had been. We had no way of knowing the setup, and the sound of our engines might tip someone off to our presence. I dropped the anchor, and Zef began to strip off his outer clothing.

"Remember, come on back once you've checked it out. If you don't, I'll come looking for you anyway, so you won't be sparing me anything."

Zef nodded. Without speaking, he dove into the water and began swimming around the point. For the next half hour, I fantasized about eating Italian food in the actual country of Italy. I also passed some time being bummed that I didn't have a passport that I could get stamped to prove I had been to Italy. On the other hand, even if I'd had my passport, it wasn't like I was going through customs.

After about forty-five minutes total, Zef returned. He climbed up the ladder on the stern and I handed him a blanket I had found on board.

"I think it is good," he said. "There is a path out of the cave; it comes out on top, but not inside a building. There is no one there to hear us."

I raised the anchor, and we motored slowly and quietly around the corner. Unlike the catamaran, our vessel was small enough to go all the way into the cave. Zef had found a flashlight on board, and he shined it ahead, directing me. Much like in Corfu, there was a rock shelf at the back of the cave that formed a sort of jetty. Zef jumped from our boat onto this and made us fast with a rope. I was glad it worked out this way – our getaway would have been terribly slow if we had been forced to swim any distance out to the boat. Plus, I didn't know if Lena or Talia could swim in the first place.

I jumped onto the rock shelf myself and followed as Zef led the way toward the tunnel.

I quickly became aware that it was more of a giant fissure in the rock of the cliff than a tunnel. I could see a thin ribbon of evening sky far above me, while the ground that I was walking on sloped steeply upwards. If I stretched out my arms, I could touch both walls of the fissure with my fingertips. As in Corfu, someone had bolted iron piping to the rock on one side, where it served as a convenient hand-rail. We went straight back from the cave for a while, climbing all the way. Then, the path began to curve gently to the right, still going up. There was a sharp left turn, and it ran level for about thirty yards, and then dead-ended in a vertical rock face that was about twenty feet high. The walls of the fissure continued on above the top of the little cliff in front of us.

"Wait," said Zef. He walked up to the rock face, and just kind of casually climbed up to the top. While I stood there, considering whether I wanted to start feeling old already, he lowered a ladder. It was just an ordinary ladder, the kind used by painters, home-owners, and human traffickers the world over.

"Handy," I said, when I reached the top.

"Yes. The cliff will keep out the tourists who wander up the path from the cave, but the ladder makes it easy when the traffickers want to bring people up from the water."

We were now much nearer to the top of the cleft. The sides rose only ten feet or so above us. Ahead, the path sloped gently up for thirty yards or so, until it was level with the surrounding ground.

"This is as far as I came," said Zef.

"Why didn't you lower the ladder when you were up here the first time?"

He shrugged. "There was a possibility that someone would come and check, and wonder why it had been lowered."

Reluctantly, I had to conclude that it was smart thinking, not showing off, which had led him to leave the ladder at the top. A thought occurred to me. "What about now?"

"I think we should leave it. We may need to get out of here in a hurry."

I nodded. "If we get the chance, we can pull it down after us. That might delay them a little if they're chasing us."

Zef nodded, and then led the way up to the top.

We were on a kind of grassy, brushy upland. It was lighter up here than it had been down in the rock cleft, but the sun was long past the horizon, and as long as we stood still, I wasn't worried about being seen. The path kept on through the grass and brush ahead of us. Maybe a hundred yards away, we could see a big building. It looked like some sort of shed or warehouse. Maybe fifty yards to the left of it was a sprawling farm house made of grey stone. The house looked very Italian and very old, spreading out in an L-shape with two wings. The shed looked like it belonged on a farm in Midwestern America. The nearest lights were several hundred yards away on either side.

We approached slowly, crouching as we moved through the grass and brush. Though it was deep dusk, I could not see any lights on in the house. When we were a mere ten yards from it, I grabbed Zef's arm. We stopped and I pointed, whispering.

"Bars over the windows."

Zef shrugged. "It is nothing. This is how it is in Europe. Nearly every building in Albania has bars on the windows, and I think it is the same in most countries. Did you not notice it in Corfu?"

When I thought about it, I realized he was right – most of the buildings I had seen in Greece had metal bars over the windows, at least on the ground floors.

Zef pointed back at the window. "I am more concerned about that." He pointed at one of the dark windows.

"What?"

"Why are there no lights?"

"I was wondering that myself. Do you have any ideas?"

"I am not certain. Let us find out."

We moved carefully and quietly up to the side of the house, keeping low. This part was the long side of the "L," and the windows were facing the sea. Zef went to one side of the window, and I took the other. He slowly brought his face close to it. After a moment, he motioned me back. We crawled until we were underneath a bush about fifteen yards away.

"It is as I thought. They have blocked the window with wood, painted grey."

"Could you see anything?"

"No." His voice seemed a little short and tense.

"Do you mean there is no glass?"

"No. There is glass. But on the inside of the glass, they have blocked the window."

"So what does that mean?"

"It means they do not want anyone to see what they are doing."

"Which is?"

Zef took a deep breath. "They will do things to the girls. They will – " he waved his hand angrily and looked out over the darkening ocean. "And this place is isolated, so no one will hear, and with the windows blocked, no one will see."

It has been pointed out to me, more than once, that I have a little bit of a habit of translating anger into physical violence. It was probably a good thing that there was no one near me just then who was involved in the whole business. I could hope, though, and I did.

"Zef," I said. "I know you want to save Lena and Talia."

214

"Yes."

"But what about the others?"

He shook his head. "Our boat is not big enough."

"But we could subdue all of the traffickers, let the other girls go free."

He looked out over the water.

"All of those girls are like Lena. I bet a lot of them have someone like you, or at least a father or mother, wondering where they are, and what will happen to them."

"We don't know how many men are in there."

"The way I feel, the more, the better."

Zef looked at me. "You are very strange for a priest."

"The Roman Catholics have an order of priests, the Jesuits, who used to be both priests and warriors. I think some of the priests in ancient Israel also served as warriors."

"You are this thing, a Jesubits?"

"Jesuit. No. But I guess in some ways, I am both a pastor and a warrior."

"This is normal, in America?"

"This is not normal, anywhere. At least, I don't know of very many. But it is who I am, and I don't think I can change it, and I'm not sure I should try to, anyway."

Zef nodded to himself. "I think I like you this way."

It surprised me that he would say that, until I remembered that criminals and scumbags were always giving me compliments. Now all I needed was a church full of mobsters, and I'd be loved by all. I'd have great job security. Plus, the offerings would go through the roof when they wanted to launder money.

He touched me on the shoulder. "Come."

We drifted slowly and quietly all along the outside of the long wing of the house, and then did the same for the shorter wing. All the windows were completely dark. We checked the big shed, but it was locked. Zef pressed his ear to the door, but after a moment, he shook his head.

"It is very quiet. I don't think the girls are in here."

The inside of the L formed a kind of courtyard. A stone wall, maybe five feet high, proceeded from the top of the long wing, so the courtyard was enclosed on three sides. There was a large front door in the middle of the long wing. The short wing looked like it was originally used as a barn or stable. Two cars were parked in open bays in this structure, and there was another door, close to the corner formed by the longer side. Possibly it was used for storage, or it might be used for living quarters. It looked like a fairly large area.

The first thing we noticed were the lights. There was a light on at the far end of the house on the ground floor. Three of the upstairs windows also showed a warm glow.

"Behind the wall," said Zef. "We can follow it until we are right next to the house, and from there, keep close and move to the door. Someone looking out from upstairs would not see us.

"And downstairs?"

"Not if the windows are blocked off."

"What about that one?" I pointed to the downstairs window that was lit.

"We crawl underneath it."

"Okay," I said. It seemed like a better option than just walking up to the door.

We swung wide and then came back toward the house, taking cover behind the stone wall that formed one side of the courtyard. Staying low, we moved until we were right next to the house again. Zef slipped over the wall like a cat. I waited a few seconds, and then I went over the wall like a slightly slower, older cat.

We were very close to the lighted window. Zef slid a cautious eye over the edge, waited a moment and then stepped silently back to me. Cupping his hand over my ear, he whispered, "The kitchen. Three men, drinking coffee."

I heartily wished that he hadn't mentioned the coffee. Well, perhaps it was all good. It gave me that much more motivation to get in there, take out the bandits, and have a nice cup of Joe while we...I realized that we wouldn't have time for coffee if we were getting Lena and Talia out of there. Rats.

Zef went ahead of me on his hands and knees, staying under the level of the window sill. I did the same. The next window was dark, but Zef cautiously looked into it anyway. He frowned, shook his head, and gestured that we should get down. I guessed that meant that this window was not blacked out by wood. There were two more windows before we reached the arched doorway in the middle, and we crawled beneath both of them.

The doorway was arched and recessed. There was nothing to do but step under the arch. The door was locked. Zef stepped back, as if he was going to kick it open.

"Wait," I said, holding up my hand. We had a brief whispered conversation, and then I went to the edge of the arch and laid down. If someone were to open the front door, he would clearly see my feet and legs, while the rest of me would be out of sight, around the corner.

Zef stepped up to the door, knocked loudly, and then quickly came around the corner and stood over me. For a moment nothing happened except that my heart began to beat very fast and loud. Then I heard the door being opened. I let out a soft groan. Steps sounded in the arched entry. A man stepped around the corner, and Zef head-butted him in the face. The man collapsed silently.

"That's called using your head," I said, as Zef helped me to my feet.

"Of course," said Zef with a puzzled expression on his face. "That is what it is. You use your head to strike your opponent."

"No, I mean, it's an expression... never mind." I was used to people who did not think my wisecracks were as hilarious as they obviously were, but it was disconcerting to have someone not even recognize that I was attempting to be funny. Language is a bear.

The front door was open, and we walked in. In front of us was a broad staircase going up. To the left was a hallway with several doors, and to the right a large room, probably the living room. Beyond it showed the light we had seen at the end of the house, which Zef had said was the kitchen. We moved quickly towards it. The plan was to find and subdue all the traffickers. Zef had seen three in the kitchen. Assuming the man Zef had taken out had come from there, we had only two more to go, and then we could go upstairs, and deal with the men there. But before we could reach the door another man stepped out, calling a question, no doubt wondering what was taking the first man so long to return. He saw us. Zef leaped for him, but the man managed to shout a loud warning before Zef's elbow crashed into his temple. I slipped behind them and confronted the remaining man in the kitchen. Even as I entered, he was scrambling to put a large wooden chopping table between us. He turned at the counter behind him, and then quickly whirled around again, holding a wicked, sharp-looking butcher knife. He was a few inches shorter than me, with dark, greasy hair and a scraggly, dirty-looking mustache. His eyes were small, and they glinted with malicious satisfaction when he saw that I was unarmed.

He made a lunge for me, but I kept the table between us, never taking my eyes off him. He was on my right, and I let him edge a little closer, and then jerked away to my left as he made another pass at me. Now I was on the side of the table opposite the door. I pretended to turn to look for another knife where he had found his. The greasy-haired man yelled with triumph, and then collapsed as Zef stepped through the door behind him and clobbered him on the back of the head.

"We make a good team," I said. "Except, I'm tired of being the bait. Next time, it's your turn."

He opened his mouth to reply, but was preempted by a voice behind him. A man stepped through the door, holding an AK-47 automatic rifle, the most common gun in the world, favored by everyone from Central American rebels to Somali pirates, and apparently, Albanian human traffickers. The man barked out a sharp command. Zef turned, and together, we slowly raised our hands.

THIRTY-FOUR

"I think we need to revise our plan a little bit," I said to Zef.

The man holding the AK-47 spoke sharply, I assumed, in Albanian.

Zef spoke to him. Just as he finished, two other men stepped inside the kitchen. One held a pistol, and the other, nothing. The unarmed man looked about thirty-five years old with dark hair, but startlingly light eyes, and he had an air of arrogant self-assurance about him. He seemed to be the one in charge of this part of the operation.

"So," he said in English, "What are you doing in this house? Why are you attacking these men?"

"It's a hobby," I said. "The latest travel craze. Americans go overseas to fight thugs. It's called combat-tourism."

The man's lips tightened. "I see you think you are a funny man."

"Well," I said modestly, "this isn't my best material. The language barrier makes it more difficult."

"You are in a great deal of trouble. Please understand that this is very serious, what you have done."

"I will say the same thing for you, from an eternal perspective. In fact, you are in much more serious trouble than me."

"Is this funny again?" asked the man, with a puzzled expression.

"Not even a little bit," I said.

He shrugged impatiently. "This is pointless. What are you doing here?"

Both Zef and I remained silent.

The light-eyed man stepped over to me without warning and drove his fist into my stomach. As punches go, I have received much worse, but I doubled over with feigned agony, groaning as if he had hurt me badly.

"I will ask you again," he said, with satisfaction in his voice, "what are you doing here? Did someone send you?"

I nodded. "At first, I think maybe I just came because I wanted to. But the more I think about it, the more I think it was God who sent me."

"There is no God," said the man. He drew his hand back for a big, hard punch. When it came, I sidestepped, grabbing his wrist and twisting it around and up with my right hand as I slipped my left around his neck. Before anyone else could react, I had his hand up between his shoulder blades, ready to dislocate the shoulder, while I held him in front of me, keeping him there with my left arm, which was locked around his neck.

"You will find out very soon if there is a God or not," I said, "unless your men put down their guns."

The man with the pistol had his gun pushed into Zef's temple, while the man the AK-47 waved his rifle uncertainly. The man I held shouted something in Albanian, and other two shouted back.

"Put down your guns," I yelled into the noise. It was an intense moment, with everyone except Zef yelling at each other, me trying to keep the leader between me and the bullets, and Zef standing rock-still, a millisecond away from oblivion.

Suddenly, there was the sound of breaking glass, and then a white light that blinded me, and the deafening roar of an explosion.

I lost my grip on the man in front of me, and fell to my knees, unable to see or hear anything. As I blinked and shook my head, hands grabbed me roughly, pulling me to my feet. My wrists were jerked behind my back and fastened together with something that felt like handcuffs. I felt barely conscious and dazed as I was marched out of the kitchen. My vision began to clear about the time we reached the courtyard. There were a dozen figures, or more, walking around purposefully. They were dressed in black and wearing black flak-jackets and helmets, holding what looked like submachine guns of some sort. Ahead of me, some of the black-clad men were helping a handcuffed man into a kind of big van, while three people stood by and watched. The person behind me pushed me roughly toward the low courtyard wall. He made me sit down with my back to the wall, at the end of a line of prisoners. I counted four men to my left. It wasn't long before Zef was pushed down next to me. Over the next few minutes, five more men were shoved into place against the wall.

Three of the black-clad men stood in front of us, holding their automatic weapons at the ready. The center one spoke loudly to us. I wasn't sure of the language, but it might have been Italian.

"Excuse me," I called, "I know it's stupid and ugly and everything, but I only speak English. Could you repeat that?"

One of the other men put his head close to the center man, and they obviously exchanged words. Then the center man called loudly over his shoulder, never taking his eyes off us.

Two more people came over to look at us. One of them was a woman with dark hair and eyes, who looked Italian.

"Him," she said in English, pointing to me. Her companion came over to me, grabbed my right arm and hauled me to my feet.

I jerked my head toward Zef. "Him, too," I said.

The woman regarded me steadily with her brown eyes. "Later," she said.

I was escorted to the other side of the big van in the courtyard, where my handcuffs were removed.

"Boy, are you a sight for sore eyes," I said to the woman. "I hate to admit it, but we sure needed the help."

She met my eyes for a few minutes. "Do you have any idea what you have got yourself into, Jonah?" said Jasmine at last.

THIRTY-FIVE

"Well, shoot, I thought you would know," I said.

She shook her head impatiently. "You never quit, do you?"

I nodded. "And, quite possibly, you're alive because of it. Never quitting was a pretty good thing out in that storm on Lake Superior."

"Fair enough. But that still doesn't answer my question. What are you doing here?"

"Well, let me go out on a limb here, and guess that you're here yourself because you finally got some hard intelligence on the human trafficking." I rubbed my eyes a little bit.

"Sorry about the flash-bang grenade."

"Don't be sorry. You people saved our hides."

Jasmine nodded her head. Her smooth dark hair gleamed in the moonlight. "We're here because Leyla got ahold of us and told us to track the cell phone that Joe Williams gave you. She said that you said you were following the traffickers."

"Actually, I gave the phone to one of the girls, precisely so you could track the trafficking operation."

"That was brilliant, except for the part about not writing my number or the number of the embassy."

"Well, I never claimed to be perfect. Or brilliant. Again, your timing was impeccable."

"Actually, we got here just before you did. We moved in right after dark. We saw you when you went inside. Nice little trick there to get the door unlocked."

"Who is 'we,' anyway?"

"Interpol. I told you, I'm on a task force."

"Why didn't you stop us when you saw us sneaking along the front of the house?"

"We weren't quite ready. And I didn't know you were going to go all Sir Galahad and try to bust up the place."

"Really? Knowing me, you couldn't have guessed that?"

"Some people change, you know. Mature."

"Listen," I said, "though your opinion of my maturity is fascinating, three things. First, the girls are here, maybe forty or fifty of them."

"Our people are already on it."

I looked at the house, where all the lights were now on and visible through the unblocked front windows. I could see Interpol officers moving through the rooms. "There's a big shed," I said, "almost a pole barn. And some sort of storage area or something there." As I turned and pointed to the corner where the house met the old barn or stable, I could see another officer prying the padlock off the door with a crowbar.

"As you can see," said Jasmine, "we've got it covered."

"Okay, second thing," I said. "The man I pointed out back there – you really do need to talk to him. His name is Zef, and he is the nephew of the kingpin – the main guy behind the human trafficking. Your big fish."

The expression on her face was gratifying. She was barely holding herself back from running over to Zef. "Thank you, Jonah, seriously. That's huge. Quickly, please, what's the third thing?

"Galahad." I said. "Seriously, why not Lancelot?"

"Shut up, Jonah," said Jasmine as she strode quickly away to find Zef.

~

I had been involved in some law-enforcement operations on previous occasions, and I expected a lot of hanging around and waiting, and a lot of telling my story over and over again. Mostly, things went according to expectations. The girls were found packed into the big storage room that was probably part of the old stable, just next to the main living quarters of the house. It was the corner room I had pointed out to Jasmine. The girls had not been hurt, and, according to what I heard from Jasmine, mostly they were upset because they had been caught sneaking into Italy. They didn't feel like they had been rescued from anything. I was disappointed and concerned to learn that Talia was not among them.

Jasmine settled me in a room in the farmhouse. It held a couch and two chairs. I wasn't sure why – it didn't really look like a living room, but maybe the traffickers had used it as a sort of den. There was nothing on the white walls, and the electric bulb above was bare. After a while, Jasmine came in. She asked me to tell her my story, and I did. She asked me a ton of questions, all of which I answered truthfully. She left again for a long time, and then returned, bringing Zef and an Interpol cop with her.

"Your stories agree," she said.

"Now may I talk to Lena?" asked Zef. He looked like he thought he had been very patient, but that now it was time for his cooperation to be rewarded.

"In a minute," said Jasmine.

"Why not now?" I said.

Jasmine looked at me with interest. "Any particular reason?"

"Yes. I'll tell you when he goes."

She looked at the Interpol cop, and then back at Zef. "He goes with you. Ten minutes."

Zef needed no encouragement. He shot out of his chair and stepped from the room, followed by the hurrying policeman.

"So what's your reason?" asked Jasmine.

"I have an idea, and we'll need his help. I think his reunion with Lena is going to go in such a way that he'll be willing to give us that help."

"Why should we need his help?"

"You don't have your big fish yet, do you?"

"This Milot of yours? No. We've hurt him, and he'll have to change his methods and routes, but we've got nothing on him, himself. He'll be back at it in a matter of months, and he'll be harder than ever to catch."

"When Zef comes back, I'll tell you my idea. I'll bet you he'll go for it."

Zef returned within the ten allotted minutes, accompanied by the Interpol man. He looked despondent.

"How did it go?" I asked.

He shook his head, and then let it hang down. I waited. Jasmine made to speak, but I waved my hand to silence her. Sometimes you need to let a silence grow in order to encourage someone to talk. Not all of my pastoral training was useless.

At last, Zef raised his head. "She does not believe me."

I stayed quiet and shot a quick look at Jasmine to keep her the same way.

"She thinks I followed her and brought the police because I am jealous. She says I do not want her to have a happy life in the EU, that I want to keep her like a slave in Albania. She says I have ruined her life."

"I'm sorry, Zef," I said at last.

We were quiet for a little while.

"It is not only about me," he said, finally. "It is her. I have not saved her; she will only do this again. And Milot; if Milot finds out, he will make sure that she will die a terrible death, in order to punish me."

I tried to keep my voice normal. "So the only way to save her is to take down Milot?"

He looked at me sharply. "I did not say this."

"But it's true, isn't it? She won't be safe unless Milot is out of the picture."

Jasmine looked at me and nodded slowly, understanding dawning in her eyes.

Finally, Zef nodded also. "What you say is true."

"Would you be willing to help us take down Milot?"

He was quiet again. "I will be killed. Even if we get Milot, the Mafia will not allow it to go unpunished. I will die." He took a breath. "But I would do it for Lena, if I can be sure it works."

"What if we worked it out so that you would be safe from the Mafia?"

He shook his head. "There is no place safe from them."

"Maybe not in this part of the world." I looked at Jasmine.

Jasmine nodded slowly, catching up with my train of thought. "We might be able to figure something out."

"Might?"

"We will."

"Lena will not come with me," said Zef. It was not a question.

"No. It would mean you would never see her again. But she would be safe."

Once more Zef retreated into his thoughts. At last he said, "I will never see her again if one of us is dead, anyway."

"So you will help us?" asked Jasmine.

"Yes."

"Okay," I said, and told them what I had in mind.

THIRTY-SIX

Jasmine arranged for an Interpol helicopter to fly me back to Corfu. It took some time to arrange, of course, but at last the big machine came to rest in the courtyard of the Italian farmhouse. The noise was unbelievable. Jasmine touched my shoulder, and I got on board. I had never been on a helicopter before, and I thought I would be excited by the experience. However, it was dark and we flew out over the ocean almost immediately, so there was nothing to see; in addition, I hadn't had much sleep over the past few nights. I fell asleep less than five minutes after we took off.

A hand on my shoulder wakened me, and I was surprised to see that we were already on the ground.

"So soon?" I shouted.

The crewman nodded. "We cruise at one-hundred and forty knots, and it was only seventy miles. You have been asleep for twenty-five minutes."

I got out of my harness and jumped out the door, ducking my head, though I knew there was no way the blades could possibly hit me. As soon as I was clear, the engine revolutions kicked up, and I had to close my eyes as dust and sand and small pebbles were hurled through the air all around me.

Twenty minutes later, I was back on my motor scooter, headed from Paleokastritsa toward Agios Georgios and Leyla. I had a hard time believing that it was only a little after midnight: in spite of my nap, I felt like I had been awake for days.

Like the night before, it was clear. I wanted to see Leyla, but I had to pause at the edge of a switchback to take in the beautiful sweep of grey-green mountainside and indigo ocean lying quiet and peaceful under the pale moon. It was anyone's dream of a Mediterranean island night.

At last I arrived, removed my helmet, and took a deep breath. "Here goes nothing," I said. I looked around once more, and then entered the house.

All was quiet and dark. I locked the door behind me, and then turned to the spare bedroom. Opening the door softly, I said, "Honey, I'm home."

A light flicked on in the living area behind me. As I started to turn toward it, something struck the back of my head. My eyes rolled back, and I fell to the floor.

~

When I opened my eyes again, everything felt different. The room seemed to be moving and swaying. As things came into focus, I realized that I was on some sort of chair, with two men standing, one on either side. I realized that one of them must have just slapped my cheek in an effort to bring me around.

Sitting in front of me was Milot. The ugly scar on the right side of his face showed up red in the bright light. There was a large white bandage/splint around his nose.

"So," he said, looking at me coldly, "you have returned to your wife, but all you find here is me." He spread his hands apologetically. "I am not as attractive, I know. But perhaps, when we are done with her, I will be the pretty one, compared to her."

I stared at him in confusion. "But what...?" I couldn't think of what to say. "How did you...?"

Milot waved a hand modestly. "It is nothing. It was no problem to find out where you were keeping her."

He was sitting directly opposite me, relaxing comfortably in a large armchair. A bodyguard was standing next to him. As far as I could tell, besides the guards, there was no one else in the room, though strange creaking sounds echoed constantly around us.

Milot was watching me with interest. "Do you think you will overcome my guards once more?" he asked. He nodded to the men on either side of me. "Perhaps you would have no problem with Tomor and Imer here – I understand from a number of my men that you are very good. But not as good, I think, as my nephew." He nodded to the man standing next to him, who was tall with short dark hair, dark eyes and the remains of a bruise below his left eye. "Zef," he said, "meet Reverend Borden. Reverend Borden, meet my nephew, Zef."

Zef nodded coldly toward me. I eyed him.

Milot spoke again. "I had to get rid of Bekim. He did not show himself very well last time you and I met." He turned to Zef. "If Father Borden attempts anything, I want you to kill him. But break as many bones as you can, first."

"Of course, Uncle," said Zef.

"How do you know he can?" I asked.

"Oh, I have no fear about that. He can."

"He'll have these two lugs to help him, of course," I said, looking at the two men next to me. Zef was starting to look a little irritated.

"Of course," said Milot.

"Milot," I asked, "Why do you do it? Why did you kidnap those girls? What did they ever do to you?"

"Well," said Milot, and then paused with a funny look on his face. Unlikely as it seemed, I would have called it amusement. "What girls are you talking about?" he asked.

"Lena, Talia – and all those others I saw in the convent in Paleokastritsa."

"Ah, the convent at Paleokastritsa. Yes, that is a beautiful place."

I was feeling a little irritated, could not help showing it. The room was still shifting in my perception. I must have been hit pretty hard. "You know what I mean. The girls that you keep there."

"Now, Reverend Borden, I am afraid you are imagining things. And such things! You are having fantasies about the nuns, yes?"

"No fantasies. You are smuggling girls, and keeping them there until you want them somewhere else."

"I have no girls," said Milot. "I am not a smuggler." His expression was one of someone being kind to an inmate in an insane asylum. "You must have me confused with a man I know named Yakov. He runs a brothel. But I? I have nothing to do with these things."

Something wasn't right. Alarm bells were going off, and I could tell that my face was showing my consternation. "All right, you tell me what was going on there, then." I shook my head to try and stop the swaying movement of the room around me.

Now I was sure that Milot's overriding mood was one of amusement. He seemed to be struggling not to laugh. At last, he let it out, an unpleasant, phlegmy series of guffaws, clearly at my expense. His shoulders still shaking, he gained control enough to speak. "Even now, you have no idea," he said. "What a pompous, useless ass you are, Father Borden."

This seemed a tad unkind, especially since just a few days earlier he had said he almost liked me.

Milot laughed again, and then gestured to Zef. "Take it off."

Zef strode over to me. "What are you doing?" I asked.

He kept coming.

"Zef?"

He stopped in front of me. My eyes widened in horror as I realized what was going on. "We had a deal," I whispered urgently. "What about Lena?"

He shrugged, his face showing its usual lack of expression. "I do not apologize, Borden. I believe you have a saying, 'blood is thicker than water.' So it is. Milot is my uncle; I cannot betray him. I am unhappy about Lena, but as you yourself said, clearly, she does not love me."

I offered no resistance as Zef jerked my shirt up over my head. I was wearing a wire – a microphone/transmitter unit – that was supposed to pick up Milot's unforced confession, and end this foul business. Zef ripped it off my body with no regard for the tape that held it there. I pulled my shirt back down and watched as he dropped it to the floor, grinding it underneath his heel.

"You are a piece of scum," I said, unable to keep the hurt and anger from my voice. Zef ignored me, and went back and stood impassively next to Milot. "They will be here any minute," I said. "They heard everything until you did that. They'll know something is wrong."

"But no, Father Borden," said Milot, still chuckling. "Even now you are too stupid. You think perhaps that the room sways because Zef hit you so hard when he knocked you unconscious before?"

I tried to contain the sickening feeling I felt as he spoke. I realized the truth before he said it.

"We are on my private yacht, anchored out in the bay. There is no one here to listen. I had men watching as we came out here, while you were unconscious. No one followed us out into the water. We were undetected." He smiled, and it was perhaps the ugliest thing I had ever seen.

"I could not resist deceiving you. The expression on your face now was worth every minute we wasted on this charade. Zef has told me everything. To think, you were going to get me to confess all my crimes into your silly little microphone." He started laughing again and let himself go for a few minutes. It reminded me of footage I had seen of hyenas in Africa. At last, he gained control of himself. "Even if I had confessed, we are out of range out here on the water." He smiled in malicious pleasure. "But of course, I will admit to my crimes now – so that you will know, before I kill you, that you have failed utterly. To know that you were right, that you had the chance, and that you failed – this is utmost humiliation."

I looked at Zef. "You said blood is thicker than water. Talia is also your blood."

His face looked troubled for a moment, but then he shook his head, as if in irritation. "I have made my choice."

"My nephew will do what I tell him," said Milot. "He is loyal to me." He smiled again, and I looked away.

He spoke sharply in Albanian, and one of the men next to me forced my head around to face Milot once more. "You will look at me when I speak to you," he said. "I will see the despair in your eyes. Yes indeed, I am the one who smuggles girls from the Middle East, Africa, and Eastern Europe into the EU. Of course, you discovered part of my operation at the convent. How does it feel to know that you can do nothing about it?"

"Rotten," I said. "I still can't believe you got a priest to go along with it."

Milot spat. "Priests are either pathetic or hypocrites. Do not worry about your professional pride."

"So which was this one?"

"Actually, it was a stroke of very good luck." Milot started chuckling again. "I just said something very funny, though you do not know it. You see, the priest in charge of the convent at Paleokastritsa had a stroke several years ago – a stroke of good luck, for me, you see. I was fortunate in that I was visiting when it happened. I had heard rumors of the caves underneath there, and I was investigating. When the priest fell ill, I was able to take charge of him and bring him to hospital. When it was evident that he would not recover fully, I bribed and threatened certain people in hospital, and called one of my men to masquerade as another priest who took him back to the convent when he recovered. The real priest was incapacitated, and my man began to run things, using the first priest as his authority. Soon we had cleared out all the nuns except one, who wouldn't leave because she wanted to care for the old priest. We kidnapped some of her family to buy her silence. As far as the church is concerned, all is well with the convent at Paleokastritsa.

They send in plenty of money from tourist donations, so no one sees the need to ask questions."

"You suborned a disabled priest? You are the mastermind of this operation."

"Indeed. Ingenious, is it not?"

"And you started shipping the girls out from there?"

"Yes. We are very kind to them until they get to Italy. That way they cooperate. We take them in a boat out of the cave, so they look like just another tourist group around Paleokastritsa. Then we put them in a bigger boat and ship them to Italy."

Milot paused and made sure I was looking at him. "Would you like to know just how badly you failed? I will tell you. In Italy, we rape the girls and beat them until they are completely broken. After that, they are obedient little prostitutes, who will do anything we tell them."

I felt sick, and this time, had no problem with letting it show. "You do this? Yourself?"

"In the beginning, yes. Now, it is mostly my men, whenever I tell them to. However, I do still indulge myself on special occasions. That is what I want you to know. I will make a special occasion this time, and I will personally participate in doing this to Talia and your pretty little wife. I want you to think about this while I slowly kill you."

"You have them? You kidnapped them?"

He shrugged. "I will have your wife before it is dawn. I have had Talia for many days, as you no doubt suspected."

"Where?"

He laughed. "The brothel where you met me before is officially run by a man named Yakov, but he is *my* man; he runs it for me and does what I say. Talia was there both times you came to see me, and you never even suspected, you are so pathetic. I will go there soon to teach her not to interfere with me."

I felt like throwing up. "Enough," I said. "I've heard enough."

Zef walked over until he was standing in front of me. "You will listen until he says you are done," he said, standing close. I met his eyes.

"My right," I said.

He nodded. There was a brief pause, and then he slammed his elbow into the temple of the man standing at my right hand side. At the same time, I launched myself from the chair, using my momentum to drive the top of my head under the chin of the man on my left. Both men fell to the floor, unconscious. I was already leaping for Milot, to silence him before he called for help. The big white bandage on his nose made an irresistible target, so I broke his nose again, then stepped back and drove a side-kick into his liver while he still sat stunned in his chair. He kind of slid out of it to his hands and knees and began retching.

"If he cannot breathe from his nose, he may possibly choke on his own vomit," said Zef.

"Don't get my hopes up," I said.

Zef looked at me. "You said you thought he was kind to me, at one time."

I was already feeling remorse before he had finished the sentence. Having morals can be embarrassing when you don't live by them, and a nuisance at times when you do, but for me, anyway, it's far better than the alternative. I ripped my shirt and then knelt beside Milot, cleaning blood and vomit from his face, making sure his airway remained clear. Once I had to stick my fingers into his mouth, but he was too far gone to bite, and I kept him from choking. I said a quick prayer for forgiveness and stayed down beside Milot until I was sure he was safe.

"Lie down," said Zef sharply.

I had just complied when someone entered the room.

Someone spoke, and then Zef responded with an urgent voice. The person stepped into the room, there was the sound of a blow, and then Zef said, "Okay."

Another man was stretched out on the floor of the cabin.

"Where are they?" I asked.

"I am not sure," said Zef. "There are only two left on board. Why don't we call them?"

Zef called out, and we took up positions on either side of the door. Zef took the first man, and I took the second.

"That's all of them," said Zef. "Five, plus you, me, and Milot." He looked down at his chest and spoke loudly. "Did you hear? We have subdued everyone." He looked over at me. "Actually, maybe you should say it. I think your friend Jasmine does not trust me still."

I walked over and aimed my voice at Zef's chest. "Jasmine, he's cool. You heard it all – he did exactly what we asked. All bandits are down. Only us two friendlies left."

Outside, I heard the roar of a powerful outboard engine, and then a bump, as another vessel contacted the side of the yacht. Feet thudded on deck, and people shouted. Then uniformed cops burst into the cabin holding submachine guns and shouting at us. We raised our hands. Everyone stood still for a moment, and then Jasmine entered.

"Sorry it took so long. With this moonlight, we couldn't send the zodiacs until you had everything, or they would have seen us coming."

Zef pulled his shirt up, and removed the recorder and transmitter that were taped to his body. He handed them to Jasmine.

She took them. "Thank you. We heard it all. You did a good job; you played your part well."

"Milot is not a good person," said Zef. "But he is my uncle. I needed to do this, but I am not sure I feel happy about it." While he spoke, officers were cuffing Milot, and then also securing the five thugs that Zef and I had rendered hors de combat.

I put my hand on Zef's shoulder. "You did the right thing. Strangely, doing the right thing is sometimes hard, and doesn't always feel great at the time."

He shrugged. "I am still not sure that you can protect me from his people."

"We'll think of something," I said.

THIRTY-SEVEN

The next day as we were having lunch on the terrace, Jasmine called on our new embassy-issued cell phone to report that most of Milot's operation had been rolled up.

"There are just one or two loose ends to wrap up, but I think we've got most of it," she said.

"What are you missing?"

"Well, the biggest thing is, we don't have the fake priest yet. His real name is Gregor. When we sent people to the monastery, they got all the hired muscle that you described, but Gregor was already gone."

"That's unfortunate."

"We'll get him," said Jasmine.

"I certainly hope so," I said. We hung up, and I gave Leyla the update.

"You know what really irritates me?" asked Leyla.

"I'm looking forward to a lifetime of finding out," I said. She ignored me.

"Our pictures."

"Our pictures irritate you?"

"Yes. I mean, the fact that we lost them. This is our honeymoon, and I had to throw away all of our pictures, just because of that stupid fake priest."

"So you want them to catch Gregor because in response to him, you threw your camera in the ocean?"

She thought for a moment. "No, I want them to get him because he is a scumbag who helped smuggle girls into sex slavery. But I'm also mad at him because of our camera."

"Good to know you have priorities," I said. "Why did you throw the camera away, anyway?"

"I'm not entirely sure. I just knew he wanted it, and I decided he wasn't going to have it."

"Why *did* he want it, I wonder?"

"I've wondered the same thing. I thought about it, after they locked me in the room up there. I think he believed I had taken some pictures of the girls that would somehow have put their operation at risk. Remember how he fiddled with the camera before he took our photograph? I think he was looking through my previous pictures, trying to see if I had anything that might incriminate him."

"That makes sense," I said, sipping some coffee-flavored foam, and wishing it were the real thing. I had an idea. I often have them when drinking coffee. When I shared that with Leyla once, she pointed out that since I'm almost always drinking coffee, it stands to reason that I would have ideas while doing it, from time to time.

"You know," I said, "maybe we can still get our honeymoon pictures."

"How?"

"Well, the camera would be ruined, obviously. But I wonder if the memory card might still be okay? Those things are pretty tough. We could put it in a bag of rice for a few days, and see if we might get the pictures off it."

"That would be worth a try," she said, "if we had the camera and card in the first place."

"We know where you threw it off the cliff," I said. "I bet the water is only about fifteen feet deep there. I might be able to dive for it."

After lunch we rented a kayak, some masks, fins, and snorkels. I also purchased a waterproof flashlight, with the idea that perhaps the camera had fallen into a crack in the rocks. We paddled around to the outside of the peninsula. I kept looking up at the cliffs, searching for the monastery, or a section that seemed familiar. At last I was pretty sure we were looking at the big pine tree that stood at the cliff's edge, just outside the monastery wall.

I slipped on the snorkeling gear and hung in the water, scanning the bottom for the camera. It was probably closer to twenty feet deep than fifteen, but it was also as clear as Lake Superior, and the bottom was easily visible.

There was a lot more area to cover than I had initially realized. After a while, I took a break and minded the kayak while Leyla swam and searched. Fifteen minutes later she pulled her head out of the water and called to me.

"Over here."

Before I could get there, she had disappeared under the water. She was a good swimmer, I knew, but I wondered if twenty feet was too much for her.

She emerged again much more quickly than I expected, triumphantly holding the camera over her head.

"Got it," she called.

I helped her back into the boat.

"It was right on top of that underwater rock," she said, "only about six feet or so down."

The sun was bright and warm, and I was dry already, and getting hot.

"Want to go back to the cave?" I asked. "For old time's sake?"

"Not really," said Leyla. "Why?"

"I'm hot, and it would be nice to cool off in the shade before we paddle all the way back. Plus, I have my waterproof flashlight. I wouldn't mind actually seeing the inside of that cave where we hid away."

Reluctantly, she agreed. As we slid into the cool shade and saw the water turn a brilliant blue, she sighed a little. "It *is* beautiful, though."

"That it is."

We got off onto the rock shelf and stretched our legs.

"Wanna check out our hideaway?" I asked after a while.

"Not really," she said. "You go ahead."

"Okay." I retrieved the flashlight from the kayak and dove into the water, under the rock wall. I left the flashlight off initially, since there was a little bit of light reflected from the bottom. Climbing up onto the shelf in the smaller cave, I clicked on the light. The cave was much as I had imagined it, a rough semicircle about twelve feet at its widest point.

I didn't have much time to look at anything, however. Less than three seconds after I clicked on the light, a wild figure leaped out of the darkness at me. I caught a glimpse of wide, staring eyes, disheveled hair and reaching arms, and then he was on me. I dropped the flashlight, and it rolled off the ledge, sinking into the

water, and we were suddenly in darkness. I was on my back, with my
assailant on top of me, and I could feel the man's fingers reaching
for my throat. I grabbed one of them, and broke it, and he screamed
in pain, momentarily shifting his weight. I lunged upward, head-
butting him in the face, and then he was all the way off me. My left
hand found his neck, and using that as a guide, I brought my right
elbow around against his head. It sounded like an axe striking wood,
and he went limp.

There was a splash, and as I whirled around light was shining on
me.

"Jonah?" It was Leyla.

"I'm here," I said.

"I saw the flashlight sink down. I wanted to make sure you were
okay."

"Bring it over here," I said.

She swam over and climbed out onto the ledge. "What's that?"
she asked in a surprised voice as the light caught part of the figure
which now lay still next to me.

I took the flashlight, and shined it on the man's face. It was
Gregor, the young fake priest. His hair and beard were no longer
neatly coiffed.

"He was in here?" asked Leyla.

"He jumped me, just as I climbed up here."

"Why didn't he just kick you in the head before you even got out
of the water?"

"I don't know. I think maybe he was asleep. I guess he's been
hiding here since Interpol raided the convent last night."

"Jonah," said Leyla, "if he knew about this place, why didn't he search for us here when we escaped?"

"I don't know," I said. "Maybe he discovered it after we left. Or maybe he wasn't with the people who came down the tunnel after us. You'd better go back, now, and call Jasmine, and get people in here. Bring me the strap off the camera, and I'll tie his hands with it, and wait here until the cavalry comes."

She shivered. "Isn't this ever going to be over?"

"I think it is now," I said.

THIRTY-EIGHT

The bright Greek sun warmed the air and scattered a million tiny diamonds across the surface of the Ionian Sea. A soft breeze rustled the palms near our table and gently ruffled my hair.

"This is fantastic," I said. "I am so glad we came to Corfu." I squeezed Leyla's hand.

"Even after all that's happened?" asked Jasmine. She was sitting next to Leyla, across the table from me. We were back at our little hotel in Paleokastritsa, having breakfast on the terrace. Jasmine had dropped by to update us, and she had brought the American embassy official, Joe Williams, along with her. Three days had passed since Milot had been arrested.

"Sure," I said. "We had sunshine, gorgeous views, great swimming, and almost got killed by the Albanian mob. Who could ask for more?"

"Explain this to me again," said Williams. "You were wearing a wire, but you *planned* to get caught?"

"It was Zef's idea," I said. "He thought Milot was too smart to just start telling me about his operation because I asked. He said that Milot would need to be taken off guard somehow."

"It was Jonah's idea," said Jasmine. "The triple-cross part of it, I mean. So we sent Zef in ahead of time, to tell Milot that we were planning to let him capture Jonah, and that the plan was for Jonah to wear a wire, and get Milot to talk. Zef knows Milot very well, and he suggested that Milot have a little sadistic fun with Jonah, and string him along for a while. He even gave Milot the idea to take Jonah out onto one of the boats in the bay, so that he could be sure he was safe. Milot didn't know that we would be in a yacht close enough to pick up the signal from a wire. He didn't see anyone follow them into the bay, because we were already in position before they even started out."

"Interpol found an empty house in Agios Georgios, near where Milot was keeping his yacht, and Zef told Milot that I was coming there to find Leyla. When I got there, Zef hit me gently, and I pretended to be knocked out. They took me out to the yacht from there."

"And then Zef exposed you," said Williams to me.

"Yes. I pretended to be shocked and betrayed. Milot was so delighted with his own cleverness that it never occurred to him that it was all planned, and that Zef was wearing a second wire. He couldn't wait to boast about all his crimes to me, just to spite me after I had failed. Zef was standing right next to him the whole time he was talking, getting every word on his wire."

"We heard it loud and clear," said Jasmine. "I think the legal team is up to ten or fifteen different crimes, multiple counts of each one. I don't handle the legal end, especially not here in Europe, but I heard him cop to kidnapping, rape, extortion, assault and battery, just to name a few. He won't be getting out of jail anytime this century."

"There are more than eighty years left in the century, and I thought Milot was around fifty already."

"Now you're getting the idea."

"So you got your big fish," I said.

Jasmine turned to look at me. "Indeed, I did, thanks to you."

"Thanks to Zef."

She nodded. "Yes. We're still debriefing him. He has been incredibly helpful."

"And you'll honor your deal."

She looked troubled. "Jonah, he's spent his entire adult life in the Albanian Mafia. He's not a good man."

"Neither am I," I said. "But I am a forgiven man."

"He doesn't subscribe to your belief system."

"Neither do you. No one is too old for a second chance."

"It's not about age. You must know that."

"What I know," I said, feeling a little heat, "is that you gave him your word. If you need to, we can say that it's about that."

She put up her hands and leaned back. "No, it's fine. I just wanted to make sure you still feel the same way."

"I do. We all owe him. A second chance is the least we can do."

"Okay. I got the message. I'll follow through. Okay?"

"Okay. Thanks."

Leyla had been sitting very quietly, holding my hand. She squeezed it now. "Just for the record," she said, "I agree with Jonah."

"Noted," said Jasmine.

At that moment, our server approached the table. She was in her twenties, with dark hair that had natural red highlights. Her blue eyes were striking. Leyla stood up and hugged her. "Talia!"

I gave the next hug. Jasmine had met her three days before, when she was rescued from the basement of the brothel, and had debriefed her. She stood and gave Talia a European-style greeting, with a kiss on each cheek.

"What are you doing here?" asked Leyla.

"I am working," said Talia.

"So soon?"

"My time was unpleasant, but Milot was too busy with you people to do anything terrible to me. I was not harmed."

"Really?" said Williams, fixing his blue eyes on hers. "Just like that?"

Talia seemed to shrink just a little bit. "No, not really. I am having nightmares, and I am very nervous. But perhaps coming back to something familiar will be good for me."

"Good thought," said Jasmine. She was writing something on the back of a business card. "This is the number of a woman you can talk to, if you need to. Interpol will take care of the cost."

"Thank you," said Talia. "Now, I do mean that I am trying to work like normal. What can I get you to drink?"

The others ordered coffee, and Talia looked expectantly at me. "You know what I really want?" I asked.

"I would like to know," said Talia.

"I want a big cup of black coffee. No foamed milk, no tiny cup. Just black coffee in a nice big mug."

"So you want café Americano?" asked Talia.

"What?"

"Café Americano. Plain black coffee in a large cup?"

"You mean they serve that here?" I asked, a terrible suspicion beginning to dawn on me.

"But of course. It is served in every restaurant."

I felt a surge of conflicting emotions: deep, deep chagrin at not having been more specific on any of the dozens of occasions I had ordered coffee; deep irritation that no one had suggested it before; and above all, an overwhelming, almost overpowering, joy at the thought of a good cup of ordinary black coffee.

"Yes please," I said. "Bring it as soon as possible."

"Oh," said Williams after we were sipping our drinks, "I need to give you these." He slapped two new shiny blue passports on the table in front of me. I picked up mine and handed the other to Leyla. She flipped through it.

"My stamps are gone," said Leyla sadly. "No Canada. No Mexico."

"They put in Greece, though," I said, looking at mine. "I guess they had to, to make it all kosher." I turned to Williams. "Thank you. Sorry for all the trouble we've caused."

"I think maybe you have done some things that are more than worth the inconveniences." He stood and shook hands with us. "I'll pick you up tomorrow at nine. I told the Greek authorities I would personally escort you all the way to your aircraft." He threw a fifty Euro note on the table. "Breakfast is on me. Leave the change for Talia, if you don't mind."

Jasmine said her goodbyes not too long afterwards, and we sat on the terrace soaking in the sunshine and views, euphoric with the taste of real coffee coursing through my system. Talia approached our table, and sat down at our invitation. After talking for a little while, we showed her the fifty Euro note.

"But it is far too much," she said.

"He wanted you to have it," said Leyla.

Talia picked up the bill and stood there, fingering it. "I must find some way to show him my gratitude."

Leyla and I locked eyes. "No! Please don't!" we both said at the same time.

THIRTY-NINE

We were sitting at Dylan's, the waterfront café in Grand Lake, drinking coffee after a long and leisurely lunch with Alex Chan and Julie, in which we had filled them in on our time in Greece. Outside, the great blue freshwater ocean stretched to the horizon, ruffled in the warm summer breeze, full of mystery and promise.

"I think we've finally cleared up your status with the Greek government," said Alex, sipping iced tea. He thought it enhanced his image as an Asian. Seeing as he was born and bred in the United States, I thought it enhanced his image as a Southerner. "Attacking the mob boss in the brothel was still a felony, or the equivalent," he went on. "But seeing as how he *was* a mob boss, and how you broke up a smuggling ring and all, they have exonerated you of all charges."

"Exonerated," I said.

"Hey, you use big words too; all the time."

"Yes, but I do it with so much more panache."

"That's one for Jonah," said Leyla, dipping a French fry in some Heinz fifty-seven sauce.

"You're biased."

Leyla shrugged, concentrating on getting the potato into her mouth without dripping sauce. She succeeded, and then looked at Chan. "So we can go back to Greece anytime we want?"

"Sure."

"Thank you, Alex," I said. "Seriously."

"You want to go back that badly?"

"Aside from all the fuss, Greece was wonderful. I'd actually like to go there sometime and have a normal vacation. Next time, though, I think I'll pack a coffee maker."

"Come on," said Leyla, "you would have been fine if you had just figured out sooner how to order it properly."

"Wait," said Julie. "You couldn't figure out how to order *coffee? You?*"

"Well, if you order coffee, they bring you a thimbleful of this brown, foamy stuff. You have to say 'café Americano' to get something like this."

"So let me get your story all straight," said Julie. She raised a finger and looked at me. "You *don't* speak Greek?"

"I never said I did." Even to my own ears, I sounded a little defensive. "The New Testament was written in a form of Greek that was spoken two thousand years ago. The language has changed a lot since then. And on top of that, I read it; I don't converse in it."

"So, like I was saying, you don't speak Greek."

"No."

She raised a second finger. "So you don't speak Greek, *and* you lost your passports."

"We didn't *lose* them," I said. "We already told you the whole thing. What happened was –"

"Yes, yes, I know. Ferry ride, Albanian mob, human trafficking, yada, yada, yada." She held up a third finger. "And on top of all this, you couldn't even figure out how to order *coffee?*"

I sighed, and threw up my hands. "No."

"That settles it," said Julie decisively. She looked severely from Leyla to me. "Next time, I am coming with you."

~

I drove south on Highway 61 for a few miles. The dark pines marched in thick ranks down the ridges to the tops of the cliffs that plunged into the lake, like green lemmings that suddenly stopped short of suicide. The wind was up, and the lake was flecked with white as far as the eye could see. I never understood how it could be, but Superior seemed to look different every single day, and yet, at any given time you might hear someone say, "that was a classic Lake Superior day," and they'd be right. Always the same, yet ever changing; that was our Lake of the Big Water.

As I drove, I thought about Corfu. The water there had been very much like Superior, and in spots, the cliffs and the pines were similar also. There was no denying the incredible beauty of the Greek island. And yet, there was a wildness about Lake Superior and the North Shore that had been missing from Corfu. Here, it felt like you were on the very edge of the world; and in terms of civilization, it was almost true. South was the endless blue of the lake, stretching to the horizon. North, if you did not navigate carefully, you were just as likely to hit the North Pole as you were any major town. Up in the hills above the lake roamed wolves and cougars and bears and moose, and there weren't many places left in the world like that.

I wasn't after wolves or moose, but I was after The Wild Turkey. I pulled up to it in about forty minutes. Like most casinos in Minnesota, this one was operated by American Indians, in this case, the Saganaga Band. Like most casinos the world over, it was much less glamorous in real life than casinos are in the movies. It was a nice enough building, with a log façade at the entrance as a tribute to its location in the northern forest, but when I went inside, I could smell the desperation, as I could in every casino I had ever been in. I walked down an aisle of slot machines, past a gray-haired woman who sat mindlessly plugging one with quarters. She had a kind of unthinking rhythm about her motions that made me think she had probably been doing it for hours, maybe days. While I watched, the machine rang a loud bell and a torrent of quarters poured out into a large receptacle. Without a change of expression, or a break in her rhythm, the woman scooped a handful of quarters up from the payout and kept plugging the machine. I wondered how far behind she was, to have such a complete lack of reaction to the payout.

Pastoring is a strange job: you're supposed to be in church, but you also go to jails and little homes, bars and ballgames and hospitals and cemeteries, fishing holes and even, occasionally, casinos. I wasn't here this time strictly because of my job, however. I was carrying a medium sized box.

I looked around until I saw an athletic-looking man of about six feet or so, wearing a nice pair of cowboy boots. His black hair was cut short, and he looked vaguely menacing, leaning against a pillar, watching a blackjack game. At this time of day, it was the only game going. He saw me, and made a signal to another man, who came over and replaced him as he walked toward me. He steered me to the bar where he ordered water, and I had coffee, Americano style. I set the box on top of the bar.

"How do you like your new job?" I asked.

"It is just fine," said Zef. "I am still getting used to working, how do you say?"

"Legally?"

"Yes. That is it. I am still getting used to not being a criminal."

"Everybody should," I said. "Still, security at a casino is in the same overall genre as the work you used to do."

"Yes, but I rarely have to fight."

"Cheer up," I said. "A big holiday weekend is coming up. I'm sure someone will get drunk and angry, and you'll get your chances."

"That is a comfort. Thank you, Borden."

"How many times do I have to tell you to call me Jonah?"

He shrugged. "I do not know. I have not been counting."

I nodded at the box. "I picked up something for you."

"Really?" said Zef. "For me?"

"Just so," I said, and then realized his way of talking was rubbing off on me. "Go on, open it."

Zef took the box and removed a cowboy hat. He picked it up in one hand, and then looked at me. "This is for me? You got this for me?"

"Yep. A kind of 'welcome to America' gift."

He put it on his head, and then looked in the mirror that was behind the bar. "I like it," he said, and then smiled broadly. It was the first time I had seen him really smile, and it transformed his face.

"I hope it isn't too strange for your employers. Now you will be a cowboy, working for some Indians."

He was looking in the mirror again, and the brim of the hat was pulled down so I couldn't see his eyes.

"You made a big sacrifice, and you left a lot behind," I said. "I hope this hat reminds you that you have much to look forward to, also."

He turned back to me. "It will," he said. "It will certainly do such things for me." He tugged on the brim so his eyes were hidden from me again. He wiped at his face a few times with his left hand. Finally, he looked up at me. "Thank you, Jonah."

~

I told Leyla about it when we were back in our snug log cabin, high on the ridge overlooking Lake Superior. We were making supper together.

"You really think he cried?"

"I don't know," I said. "The man is not without emotion. He cried about Lena, too."

"He's kind of a complicated man, isn't he?"

"Certainly more so than most people are likely to realize at first." I started to slice an onion. "I think I'm going to cry too."

Leyla ignored me. "Do you think he'll be all right?"

"I hope so. We can help him, can't we? Have him over for dinner and things like that."

"I think so," said Leyla, "though I never expected to have an Albanian mobster to our house for dinner."

"Ex. *Ex*-Albanian mobster." The onions were done, and I opened a jar of Kalamata olives. I wasn't sure what Leyla was doing, but as she moved around the kitchen, she kept brushing very close to me. I had thought our kitchen was bigger than that.

"Whatever."

"And I could take him fishing," I said. I thought I pulled off the casual tone pretty well.

"Zef likes to fish?" asked Leyla, suspicion in her voice.

"Didn't I tell you? When we were watching the traffickers, we had to fish for a while, as an excuse to hang around. Zef loved it."

"Jonah Borden, are you telling me you went fishing when people's lives were at stake?" She took a step towards me.

"Why do you sound so upset? It was in the cause of justice." I could smell her perfume as she stood very close, looking up at me.

"I just don't know what to do with you, sometimes," said Leyla. She was pressed up against me now.

"Really? I thought you knew exactly what to do with me," I said, my voice a little hoarse.

"Oh? I'm glad you noticed," she said, and slid her arms around my neck as she kissed me.

THE END

Did you enjoy this book?
Would you like to see more like it?
You can help!

The *Lake Superior Mystery* series depends upon you, and others like you, to keep it going and growing!

- If you haven't already, check out the other books in the series. So far we have *Justice, Storm, Secrets* and *Getaway*.
- Also check out my young adult fantasy: *The Forgotten King*.
- Post about the book, and link to it on Facebook, Twitter, LinkedIN and other social networking sites.
- Review it on Amazon, GoodReads and anywhere else people talk about books. I know I have a lot of reviews, but they all came from someone like you, and seriously, the more the better.
- Tell your friends and family about it. Blog about it.
- Sign up to get emails when new books are released by Tom Hilpert:
  http://eepurl.com/PtO61

Follow Tom Hilpert on Facebook and Twitter (@TomHilpert) Go to his webpage: www.tomhilpert.com, and sign up to receive emails when new books are released. (or use the link above). His blog is http://fictionwritersblog.wordpress.com

Author's Note

I realize that I went a little bit "edgier" in this book than in my previous novels, at least in regard to the sex-trafficking element of the story. I know that most of you read for entertainment, and I am happy to write books that are primarily for enjoyment. Even so, to make this plot work, I had to include a tiny little bit of the darker side. If it bothers you, I say, good: it should bother everyone. The life that millions of girls are forced into around the world is absolutely appalling, and nothing in this book captures anything even remotely as horrifying as the reality of sex-trafficking.

I have some friends in law enforcement who are doing something about it. Their real-life stories are heartbreaking. I'm not sure how much we ordinary citizens can do about the *legal* part of it, other than raise awareness. But I know of a group that is trying to do something to help girls have someplace to go in order to get out of their terrible situations. They are called *Courage Worldwide*, and I have friends who work with them. Here's a useful quote that tells you more about them:

> They give a girl a chance to make the courageous choice to run away from her trafficker, because there will be a loving circle of arms to fall into. Statistics are pretty brutal when it comes to victims who have managed to escape their traffickers: without strong institutional help and support, there is a very strong chance they will be retrafficked within days. Courage Worldwide has rightly

focused on the most dire need: the individual nurturing of these young people back to health and self-belief, using love as the mightiest tool of all to vanquish the evil they have experienced. They are quite literally saving young lives, lifting them back up to the light.

Courage Worldwide is at the forefront of what I hope one day will be a ubiquitous national and international movement, that of capacity-building to receive the incredibly needy and under served population of youth and adults who have been the victims of human trafficking.

—Mira Sorvino, United Nations Office on Drugs and Crime Goodwill Ambassador to Combat Human Trafficking

I encourage you, if that part of the story made you uncomfortable, go to their website and check them out: www.courageworldwide.org

Acknowledgements

I suppose it is natural to wonder if I have actually been to Corfu. The answer is, of course, yes – I spent a week there, not too long ago. It is indeed a fabulous place to visit, and I ran into no criminals while there. I will add for legal purposes that any resemblance in this book to any actual person or business establishment is purely coincidental and unintended. All events, people, and legal entities in this book are purely fictional. In any case, I want to thank two real people – Daryl and Debbie Snyder – for being instrumental in getting us to Greece and Albania in the first place.

As always, I want to thank the Ultimate Author, for giving me stories to tell, and letting me tell them, though very imperfectly.

I also need to thank (once more) Kari, Noelle, Isaac, Alana and Elise, for putting up with me all those days and nights when I sat in my room with the door closed, or said "Just give me another half hour or so."

To my readers, I highly recommend my wife Kari's music: www.karihilpert.com. If you want to know what I sound like, at least when singing, listen to the harmonies on our albums.

As usual, I owe many thanks to the League of Literary Gentlemen, a grandiose name for our humble little club: Mark Cheathem, Michael Kosser and myself. Your feedback and encouragement is vital to me. Thank you also, for putting up with my insecurities, which so often masquerade as conceit. As always, any correctly placed commas are due to Mark, and all errors my own fault. I highly recommend to you, my readers, that you Google-search each of these names, and check out their writing also. The book that Leyla read, by Mark Cheathem, is real.

Lyn Rowell, as always, provided much-needed, extremely valuable feedback on the story. I always feel a little bad that the book you read is not as good as the book everyone else gets to read, thanks to your help. Thank you, again, Lyn!

The cover design was done by the lovely and talented Lisa Anderson, who happens to be married to my cousin, Matt. Lisa is a talented photographer, and a brilliant designer. Just this past year, we finally got her to actually read a Superior novel; apparently the verdict was good. Check out more of her work at http://www.opinedesign.com

I have more encouragers, supporters and fans than I can tell, and I owe thanks to each one of you for keeping me going. Without you, there would not have been a fourth *Lake Superior Mystery*. Keep it up, **spread the word to others**, and perhaps we'll have a fifth!

Odds and Ends

A JONAH BORDEN WEBSITE

Learn more, keep up with news, and sign up for *infrequent* informational emails at www.tomhilpert.com

If you sign up for the email list, I promise I won't give your email to anyone else.

A JONAH BORDEN RECIPE – Genuine Greece-style Greek Salad.

When we were in Greece, we ate only at restaurants, or our hotel. Some of the food was terrific, some less so, but I didn't find much I could easily reproduce, except this. All ingredients readily available in the US.

Roma tomatoes, chopped.

Cucumber, sliced, and/or chopped.

Red Onion, sliced, cut slices into quarter and separate pieces.

Green Peppers, sliced thin. If desired, cut slices in half.

Kalamata olives, pitted. *These taste a bit like something in between a black and green olive.*

Feta Cheese. *For maximum authenticity, try to find it in a way that you can use a chunk about the size of a deck of cards, but maybe half as thick. If you really don't like feta, or it is unavailable, slices of parmesan also work (not shredded or powdered).*

Olive oil.

Vinegar. *I use Balsamic vinegar myself – I think the flavor works very well.*

Mix all vegetables and cheese in a bowl. Add oil and vinegar to taste. *I prefer less oil and more vinegar.*

A JONAH BORDEN PLAYLIST

I didn't get to make music as much part of this story as normal, even so, here is a selection of the kinds of songs Jonah was playing in his head during the down times:

Mona Lisas and Mad Hatters – Elton John

The Cave – Mumford & Sons

1812 Overture – Tchaikovsky

Down in the Valley – The Head & the Heart

Michigan – the Milk Carton Kids

You Draw Me In – Donna Brooks

A JONAH BORDEN MINISTRY

Some of my fans have said, in one way or another, that they wish there was a real pastor like Jonah Borden, or that there were churches where Christians like him really hung out together.

I want to assure you, I know many living Christian people who share Jonah's values and commitment to being authentic. It takes more time to get to know real people than it does to read about a character in a book, so you might have to give it time and patience. But Christians like Jonah are out there, all over the place. My own ministry association, the Alliance of Renewal Churches (http://www.allianceofrenewalchurches.org/) is full of people who would fit right in to a Jonah Borden novel.

No one is exactly like Jonah Borden, of course, not even me. But one of my passions in writing his character is that I want people to know there are, in fact, many Christians who are a lot like him. If you really want to find fellowship with such people, I humbly suggest you ask God to help you. After that, the ARC website (above) is one place (but not the only one) you might start.

I try to keep my preaching separate from my writing, because I don't want my readers to become too disappointed, or my listeners to have fictional expectations. If you think you're ready for the potential let-down, and you are truly interested, you can hear me preach at http://revth.wordpress.com

About the Author

Tom Hilpert grew up in the tropical paradise of Papua New Guinea. When he was ten years old, he knew he wanted to write books. In fact, he began writing several novels at that age. Thankfully, they are lost forever.

However, his more recent works are available in print and ebook formats. His fiction features strong, memorable, quirky characters who face mysteries and adventures with humor and persistence.

Hilpert has visited more than 17 countries, and has lived in three of them. In the U.S., he has lived in six different states, including Minnesota, the setting for the Lake Superior Mysteries. Currently, he lives in Tennessee with his wife, children, and far too many pets and farm animals.

The picture here was taken in Paleokastritsa, Corfu, Greece.

Learn more at http://www.tomhilpert.com

Like Tom's Facebook page here: Tom Hilpert's Facebook Page

CPSIA information can be obtained
at www.ICGtesting.com
Printed in the USA
LVHW041457050319
609568LV00016B/993/P

9 781519 501653